Garage Sales Can Be Fatal – A Senior Sleuthing Club Cozy Mystery – Book 2

by

Jinty James

D1523226

Garage Sales Can Be Fatal – A Senior Sleuthing Club Cozy Mystery – Book 2

by

Jinty James

ISBN: 9798859329212

DEDICATION

To my wonderful Mother, Annie, and AJ.

CHAPTER 1

What do you think about having a garage sale?" Martha asked one February afternoon.

Pru Armstrong had just arrived home from the library, and was looking forward to sitting down for a second. Her job as assistant librarian had been particularly busy that day, shepherding the local schoolchildren around the library and reading a story to them about a frog eating cupcakes.

Sinking down onto the yellow sofa in the small faux Victorian duplex, she smiled at her roommate – and friend. When she'd arrived in the small town of Gold Leaf Valley in November, becoming Martha's roommate had been the only housing option – unless she wanted to stay permanently at the local motel – but it was surprising how well they got on, even factoring in her liking for orderliness, and Martha's penchant for untidiness.

"It could be a good idea," she replied. "But I don't think I have anything to sell." She'd arrived with two suitcases and not much else.

"Goody." Martha grinned, her gray curls springing around her face. "Because I've already signed up to take part in Father Mike's church sale, and I hoped you would help me."

"Of course."

"Ruff!" *Goody!*

Teddy, the small, white, fluffy dog Martha had adopted from the animal shelter, trotted over to her, placing his paw on her knee in approval.

"I've nearly paid off my credit card," Martha continued, "but I have some old stuff I could try and sell at this garage sale and make some extra money."

She'd told Pru when they'd first met that she'd gotten into a little credit card debt going overboard buying lots of toys, bedding, and collars and leads matching her outfits when she'd first adopted Teddy. That was why she'd looked for a roommate.

"Like what?"

"Cook books for one," Martha replied. "And some odds and ends like these magnets that have fake flowers attached to them. My sleeve catches them when I'm at the fridge and they fall off, and then I have to bend down and pick them up. That sort of thing."

Pru remembered seeing the pink flowers on the fridge last week. But had they been there this morning when she'd gotten milk out of the fridge for her cereal? She didn't think so.

"I've already started sorting out some stuff." Martha gestured toward the hall, where the bedrooms were. "Father Mike's only charging five dollars per table. My friend Noreen told me about it this morning after you left for work. It's on Saturday."

"This Saturday?" Pru blinked. That was only four days away.

"Yeah, it is short notice," Martha agreed, "but Noreen told me Father Mike is worried he doesn't have enough money for the food baskets for people who need them. With all this inflation, the church funds don't go as far as they used to, and there are more parishioners than ever who need some help."

"I understand." In the last few months, additional people had joined the library which had delighted her, and her boss, Barbara, who'd muttered that it was good for their statistics.

"It starts at nine a.m.," Martha continued, "and goes 'til one. I hope Annie, Lauren, and Zoe can attend. Because that's the same time the café is open on Saturdays."

"I hope so, too," she replied. Annie was a Norwegian Forest Cat who seated the customers at the charming café. Lauren baked the wonderful cupcakes, and she and her cousin Zoe made the great lattes and cappuccinos.

"I thought we could both man the table," Martha said.

"Of course." Pru smiled.

"And it will be a great day out for Teddy."

"Ruff!" *Yes!* He stared up at Pru, a hopeful look in his eyes.

"Do you want to play in the yard?" she asked him.

"Ruff!" *Yes!*

"I took him out there this morning." Martha patted the handle of her rolling walker, which stood next to the sofa. "But then I had to sit down on this thing when I tossed the ball to him. He brought it right back to me." She grinned. "He's such a good boy."

"He is," Pru agreed.

Teddy wagged his little tail.

"I can't believe he's already ten months old," Martha said. "I really need to see if I can get him approved as an emotional support dog. Then I can take him everywhere with me!"

"Ruff!"

***

That evening, Pru helped Martha sort out more items. Some older sweat pants and matching tops that she didn't want anymore, some old socks with holes in them, (Pru didn't think anyone would want to buy them but tactfully didn't mention that) and a whole load of cookbooks which Martha said were too complicated and used too many ingredients.

Pru peeked inside one and found herself agreeing. Ten spices were listed for just one recipe, plus some other exotic ingredients she wasn't sure would be available at the local supermarket.

"Hopefully I can sell some of this stuff," Martha said at the end of the sorting out session. "Even if I can't, the table fee is going to a good cause, and maybe Father Mike will want all this." She waved her hand at the pile of books and clothes.

"What would he do with it?"

"He could give it to the people he delivers the food baskets to," Martha declared. "Maybe they're good at crafts and could do something with these socks and sweat pants." Her eyes lit up. "They could make dog toys and dog vests with them."

"You could, too," Pru encouraged.

"But you saw how long it took me to make Teddy a decent bandana a few months ago." Martha pouted. "And I haven't made another – yet. Ooh, maybe I'll see some cute fabric at the garage sale someone doesn't want, and I can buy it for Teddy. Then I could try making him another bandana."

"That's a good idea."

"Ruff!" Teddy looked up from under the pile of sweatpants.

"I wondered where you'd gotten to." Martha chuckled. "I bet you had lots of fun in there."

"Ruff!" *Yes!*

CHAPTER 2

The day of the garage sale was sunny and quite mild for February. Teddy looked cute wearing his scarlet bandana, and stood patiently while Pru buckled his turquoise lead.

"All set." She smiled at him, and his button brown eyes sparkled back.

"Let's go!" Martha pushed her rolling walker toward them in the hall. Wearing turquoise sweatpants and matching sweater, she looked ready for a day of haggling and catching up with her friends.

They'd packed Pru's car last night – or at least, Pru had. Martha had placed everything into boxes, and put sticky price labels on everything when Pru had been at work yesterday.

"Ruff!" Teddy led the way to the car.

"I don't want to get there too early," Martha said as Pru accelerated down the quiet street lined with Victorian era houses and a few replicas, "but I don't want to get there too late, either."

"I understand." She nodded.

"We might miss out on customers if we're tardy!"

A few minutes later, Pru pulled up in the church parking lot. She was lucky to snag a space, as there were plenty of vehicles parked already.

"It's just after eight-thirty." Martha peered through the windshield. "I didn't think there would be that many people here already."

"Neither did I," Pru replied ruefully. She hoped they'd have enough time to set up the table before their first customer arrived – if they got any.

Since the weather had been unseasonably warm lately, Father Mike had decided the tables should be set out on the lawn in front of the church. Pru had to admit the scene looked picturesque, although busy, with white plastic tables gracing the green grass in front of the cream painted Victorian church. A steeple perched on one side and stained-glass windows gave it a picturesque effect.

"Martha!" Father Mike, the priest of the Episcopalian church, hurried over to them as Pru got Teddy out of the car. "You're table number five."

"How many tables are there?" Pru asked the balding, middle-aged man.

"Fifteen," he replied. "If I shop carefully, that should provide another eight food parcels."

"Here." Pru dug out her wallet and handed him a five-dollar bill. "I hope this helps."

"You didn't have to do that." He smiled, accepting the cash. "But thank you."

"Ruff!" Teddy wagged his tail.

"How's your cat, Mrs. Snuggle?" Martha inquired.

Pru had learned that Father Mike had adopted a white Persian and former show cat a while ago, and although Mrs. Snuggle had a grumpy disposition, his kindness and goodness had won her over, and she was now devoted to him.

"She's good," he replied. "She had a playdate with Annie last week, which went well. But today she's relaxing on the couch while I'm out here. Although, she might decide to peek through the window of the parsonage and see if anything interesting is happening out here." He gestured to the white clapboard house next to the church.

"I can just imagine her doing that," Martha replied. "If I notice her looking out, I'll wave to her."

"She might like that," he replied in all seriousness.

Another car pulled up. Father Mike said goodbye, and headed to the newcomers, checking his notepad.

"I'll find our table, and you can start bringing the boxes," Martha said. "Wait – I can probably fit a smaller box on my walker."

"Ruff!" Teddy agreed, looking in wonder at all the people bustling here and there.

"Teddy is going to have a great day." Martha grinned. "There will be lots for him to see."

"There certainly will be," Pru agreed, glancing around.

"Hey – any sign of Detective Hottie?" Martha chuckled.

Pru hesitated. "Jesse?"

"Who else?"

"No." She shook her head. She'd met Jesse late last year, when she and Martha were on a mission to solve the book club murder, but hadn't bumped into him since. Not if you counted spotting him down the street and *making sure* she didn't bump into him.

"Too bad." Martha peered at Pru's face. "You're not wearing that lipstick I made you buy. You need to make an effort – or at least a little one since you're cute already with your auburn hair – if you want to catch him."

"Who said I wanted to catch him – or anyone?" Pru frowned.

"Smart girl." Martha nodded in approval. "Let him catch you. Yeah. You do that." She wagged a knowing finger while Pru dumped a small box on the black padded seat of the walker, hoping she wasn't blushing.

Martha trundled off in the direction of the tables, while Pru wrangled a larger box, holding Teddy's leash the whole time.

"You might have to lead me to Martha," she told him.

"Ruff!" *I will!*

"Pru! Over here!" Martha waved madly from behind a table surrounded by its neighbors.

Teddy towed her over, and sniffed at the table leg.

"Look, Father Mike's provided chairs as well, so we don't have to stand all day. I'd planned on sitting on my walker." Martha sat on one of the plastic chairs.

"Oh, good." Pru was secretly relieved as sometimes she had to stand for a while in the library, shelving books, pushing furniture around for conversation groups, and finding novels for patrons. She loved her job but it was also good to sit occasionally.

Dumping the box on the table, she noticed Martha had already set out pairs of holey socks and some of the cookbooks.

"You get another box, and I'll arrange these," Martha ordered. "Teddy can stay with me."

"Ruff," he agreed, looking up from a blade of grass.

"Okay." Pru hurried back to the car, smiling when she spotted Doris, who worked at Gary's Burger Diner.

"Hi!" Doris smiled, her arms full of clothing. She wore jeans and a slightly faded green sweater, and looked around forty. "Do you have a table as well?"

"Yes, with Martha," she replied.

"I'm table seven."

"We're five."

Doris waited while she grabbed a box from the trunk, and they walked back together.

"How's the reading going?" Pru asked. Doris had been a member of their ill-fated book club a few months ago, and had discovered a new love of books.

"It's good. I'm up to the seventh book in the Aunt Dimity series, but

I've been doing extra shifts lately at the diner as someone quit at Christmas, so I haven't been able to visit the library as often to get books."

"I understand," she replied. "I hope you can stop by soon."

"Me too." Doris nodded. "Gary's supposed to be hiring someone this week, so I hope they work out."

They reached the tables, the air buzzing with conversation. Their fellow garage salers set out their items, walking around the table and studying the effect, moving a few things here and there, and then scrutinizing them again.

"Good luck for today," Doris said. "I hope I can sell a lot of my stuff, but the money from the extra shifts is a big help right now."

"Good luck to you, too." Pru smiled at her, before depositing the contents of the box onto the table – not that there was much room left.

"Are you sure you can fit all this stuff on here?" she asked Martha.

"No problem." Martha grinned. "Some of the books might have to be piled on top of each other and people can rummage through them. That's what will probably attract customers anyway. It will be like a treasure hunt!"

"Did someone say treasure?" A slim girl in her late twenties, with a brunette pixie cut, stopped by their table.

"Ruff!" Teddy greeted her, his tail wagging.

"I hoped you'd be here, Zoe," Martha said, "but what about the café?"

"The café is opening at nine-thirty as usual, but Lauren said if we don't get many customers, we can close early and come over. But—" she turned her head this way and that, eyeing all the people, "—maybe we should have paid for a table and sold cupcakes."

"That's a great idea!" Martha's eyes lit up. "What's Lauren baking today?"

"Red velvet, super vanilla, and mocha."

"Yum!"

"We could put some away for you and bring them over when we close the café at lunchtime," Zoe offered. "I have to dash back so Lauren can come over and have a quick look here before we open up."

"Goody!" Martha beamed. "I'll have a … red velvet. Or a mocha. Hmm. Maybe I should get both."

"And I'll have a super vanilla," Pru put in. It was one of her favorites – the surprise buttercream filling inside, and a swirly dollop of frosting on top with a dusting of vanilla bean powder.

"Goody. Then we can have half each of them all." Martha eyed her hopefully. "If you want to?"

She'd wondered if Martha was going to make that offer, as they'd done it before.

"Sounds good," she replied, stifling a smile.

"Awesome!" Zoe grinned. "I'll go back to the café now and set them aside for you."

She waved goodbye, and headed toward the parking lot. Pru noticed that a couple of people stopped and spoke to her, and Zoe responded by writing something on her hand.

"What is she doing?" Pru murmured curiously.

"Probably selling more cupcakes," Martha chortled. "She's right. They should have bought a table here and sold their treats."

Pru and Martha continued setting up. Teddy attracted attention to their table, and just after nine o'clock, Martha sold one of her old cookbooks for a dollar.

"Goody." She placed the bill into an old zippered pouch slung around her waist.

Pru noticed it had been the cookbook with the complicated ingredients, and silently wished the purchaser well.

"Hey, there's Hans." Martha stood and waved madly. "Yoo hoo, Hans!"

A sixty-something dapper gentleman with gray hair strolled over to them. "Ach, Martha, it is good to see you." He smiled.

"Ruff!" Teddy sniffed Hans's trousers, his tail wagging.

"And you too, Teddy." He bent down stiffly to stroke him on the shoulder.

"Pru, this is Hans, one of Annie's regular customers at the café," Martha introduced them. "I don't think you've met."

"No, we haven't." She smiled at him. "It's nice to meet you."

"You, too." Hans's faded blue eyes twinkled. "Martha has told me you are a librarian."

"Assistant librarian," she replied.

"But one day she's going to be the head honcho of the Gold Leaf Valley library and probably all the libraries in California," Martha said proudly.

"I hope so," she replied. Her goal was to become a library director – in the distant future – but she guessed it didn't hurt to dream as big as Martha.

"Oh, guess what, Hans?" Martha barreled on without waiting for an answer, a grin forming on her lips. "The vet said Teddy is a Coton de Tulear! Just like Pru told me he might be."

"That's great!" Pru said.

"I forgot to tell you this week, what with getting ready for the garage sale." Martha waved her hand over the table laden with her odds and ends.

"Does that mean he is a pure-bred dog?" Hans asked.

"You betcha!"

"Ruff!" Teddy looked up, knowing he was being talked about in a positive way.

"That is *wunderbar*, Teddy." Hans smiled down at the fluffy white dog.

"Ruff!"

"Not that I would love him any less if he wasn't a Coton," Martha continued. "I fell in love with the little guy as soon as I met him."

"So did I," Pru admitted.

"He is a very good dog," Hans praised. "And it is so nice to see him and Annie sit together in the café."

"They're good friends," Martha said proudly.

"Ruff!" *We are!*

They chatted for a few minutes more, then Hans said goodbye and strolled over to the next table. A couple of customers came over and looked at everything of Martha's, even the holey socks, but didn't buy anything.

"Pooh," Martha murmured when they had gone.

"At least you've sold something," Pru pointed out.

"Yeah, but I don't really want to take any of this stuff back home." She eyed Pru. "Do you?"

"Not really," she admitted, "but it's your stuff."

"Maybe Father Mike will want it," Martha said hopefully.

A curvy girl around thirty came over. Her hair was light brown and shoulder length with hints of natural gold, and her eyes were hazel. She held a lavender leash with a large, silver-gray tabby walking happily on it.

"Lauren," Martha greeted her. "And Annie, of course. Hi, cutie pie."

"Brrt," the Norwegian Forest greeted them, looking around with wide green eyes.

"Ruff." Teddy gently patted Annie's shoulder with his paw. She returned his pat.

"They're saying hello to each other," Martha marveled.

"Hi, Pru." Lauren smiled. "How's it going so far?"

"Martha has sold a cookbook already."

"That's great!" Lauren checked her white wristwatch. "I have to get back to the café in a minute, although we might not have a lot of customers if everyone is over here." She glanced around at the locals greeting each other, standing in small groups talking, and browsing the tables.

"And you usually sell out of cupcakes on Saturday morning," Martha commented.

"We do." Lauren sighed. "Maybe we should have signed up for a table here instead."

"That's what Zoe said," Pru said.

"She's bringing us cupcakes at lunchtime," Martha added.

"That's right." Lauren nodded. "And Zoe got some more orders on the way back to the café."

"Annie! Teddy!" A little girl with blonde curls ran up to the fur babies. She wore a yellow smocked top over pale pink jeans.

"Brrt!" Annie greeted her.

"Ruff!"

"Hi, Molly." Lauren smiled at her.

"Hi, Lauren." Molly sat down on the grass. Teddy promptly plunked himself down on her lap, making room for Annie, who did the same.

"Sorry about that. I couldn't stop her." Claire, her mom, joined them. Tall, slim, and athletic, her hair was the same color as her daughter's, and she wore yoga pants and a blue T-shirt.

"It's okay," Lauren said. "Annie loves spending time with her."

"So does Teddy," Martha added.

"Annie, Teddy, Teddy, Annie." Molly giggled, her face alive with joy, patting both fur babies at once. "Kitty should be here!"

"She's at home relaxing and waiting for you to come home so you can play together," Claire told her.

Pru knew that Kitty was Molly's cat, who looked very similar to Annie, and that the little girl had fallen in love with her at an adoption day the café had held a while ago.

A low buzz sounded and Lauren opened her small purse. "Sorry." She glanced at the screen. "Zoe is wondering where I am."

"With me!" Molly giggled some more.

"Do you have to get back to the café?" Claire asked.

"I'm afraid so," Lauren replied.

Molly said goodbye to Annie, promising to visit her next week after school.

"She'll like that," Lauren assured Molly.

"Brrt!"

Lauren waved as they left, Annie leading her out of the church garden and back to the café.

"You can still play with Teddy," Martha told Molly.

"Ruff!" *Yes!*

Claire ended up buying an Indian cookbook from Martha, who offered it to her for free, but Claire insisted on paying.

"Tandoori chicken looks interesting." Claire flicked through a few more pages. "And I could make my own naan bread."

A few minutes later, Claire and Molly said goodbye, the little girl giving Teddy a gentle hug.

A few minutes later, Pru's attention was pulled from one of Martha's cookbooks she'd picked up.

"Yes, you did steal it!" A man's voice sounded a few tables away. "Don't try to pull the wool over my eyes. I know it was you!"

"What's going on?" Martha turned her head to the right.

"I did not steal it, and I resent the accusation." A woman's voice.

"Ruff?" Teddy looked up at Pru and Martha.

"It's okay, little guy," Martha said. "They're arguing about something, nothing to worry about."

"Why don't I take a look?" Pru offered.

"Good idea." Martha nodded, stroking Teddy.

Pru walked over to the table where the couple were arguing. A man who looked to be in his sixties with a red face and slightly uneven gray hair combed back from his widow's peak, and a woman who looked around the same age, stood facing each other. The woman had her hands on her hips behind the table, her short silver-gray hair a little disheveled, as if she'd run her fingers through it.

"This is definitely my blue shepherdess." The man picked up the statue. A graceful lady wearing a Victorian style blue gown held a lamb.

"It's mine." The woman glared at him.

"This is a rare antique," the man insisted. "And you know I got burgled last month. Yet here you are, selling *my* statue!"

"It is *not* your statue," the woman's voice held a hint of weariness.

"Is everything okay?" Pru wasn't sure what else to say, but she was aware of more people gathering around them.

"No, it isn't, miss." The man turned around and scowled at her. "Peggy here burgled my house last month and is selling my valuable statue!"

CHAPTER 3

"How dare you!" Peggy gasped. "I did *not* burgle you."

"What's going on, folks?" Father Mike hurried over, concern written on his face. By now, a large crowd circled the table.

"Father Mike, please do something about Victor," Peggy requested. "I won't have him accusing me of burglary."

"Victor, do you have any proof?" Father Mike frowned. "Maybe we should take this … disagreement … into the church office."

Victor stubbornly shook his head. "This blue shepherdess is mine. And she stole it." He jerked his thumb at Peggy.

"Father Mike," Peggy said, "if you turn over the statue, you'll see a small P in the middle. That shepherdess has been in my family for years, and one day when I was young, I got a marker and wrote my initial on it. My mother was mad, and made me promise I wouldn't do it again. But now I'm glad I did, because it proves that I'm the owner."

Victor reluctantly handed the item over to Father Mike who turned it over. "Yes, there is a small black P on the bottom," he said quietly.

"But … but …" Victor spluttered. "How? I have one exactly the same."

"Does it have a P on the bottom of it?" Father Mike asked.

"No, but how does that explain how she's got one just like mine?" His eyes narrowed. "Wait a minute. You wrote that P on the bottom after you stole it from my house!"

Peggy sucked in a big breath. "How dare you! After all I've put up with over the years living next door to you. You hate it when my grandkids come over to my house and play, and you refuse to return their balls when they ask. I have to come over and ask you to give them back. And you refuse to cut your over-hanging branches, so I have to, even though it's easier for you to do it."

"Folks." Father Mike held up his hands for quiet. "Unless you want to bring the police into this, I believe this statue belongs to Peggy." He handed it to her.

"But that's a valuable antique," Victor protested.

"No, it's not," Peggy replied. "I looked it up online a few weeks ago when I was decluttering and unfortunately it was mass produced. It has the manufacturer's mark on the bottom as well." She held it out to Father Mike to check.

"Peggy is right," Father Mike said after peering at the base of the shepherdess.

"Let me see." Victor grabbed it from Father Mike. "I'm going to look it up right now."

"Go ahead," Peggy told him. "And then you can apologize."

A few minutes later, after staring at his phone screen, Victor handed the statue back to Father Mike. "Sorry," he muttered.

"What was that?" Peggy leaned forward and held one hand behind her ear. "I didn't hear you."

"Sorry!" Victor shouted.

The remaining crowd clapped. Someone cheered.

"Here you go, Peggy." Father Mike handed the shepherdess back to her. "I apologize about this." He frowned at Victor. "I hope the rest of the day makes up for this misunderstanding."

"Thank you, Father," Peggy replied. She tucked the statue into her tote bag behind the table. "On second thoughts, I don't think I will sell her, after all. Not after what she's been through right now."

A few people applauded, then the crowd broke up and drifted over to other tables.

"But what about me?" Victor complained. "I was burgled."

"Did you report it to the police?" Father Mike asked.

"Yes."

"Then I'm sure they're dealing with it," the priest replied. "Let them do their job."

"They should have caught the criminal by now."

"Why don't you call and ask them for an update?" Peggy spoke, a mischievous tone in her voice. "And harangue them like you just harangued me?"

"I think you should return to your browsing," Father Mike advised him.

Victor nodded shortly, and stalked off.

Pru smiled sympathetically at Peggy, and returned to Martha.

"Well?" Martha asked eagerly. "I heard some of it, but fill me in on the rest."

Pru did so, watching Martha's eyes widen.

"The nerve of that man!" Martha fumed. "I've heard that he can be difficult, but to accuse his neighbor of something like that! Peggy visits the senior center sometimes, and she's a nice lady. She wouldn't burgle anyone!"

"Of course she wouldn't." A newcomer walked up to them. Her hair was a warm caramel brown, and she wore dark slacks with a cornflower blue sweater. Smiling at them, she continued, "I've known Peggy for years. I just wish I'd taken her advice and said no when Victor asked me on a date."

"He did, Cynthia?" Martha's eyes widened even more. "I heard he was a confirmed bachelor."

"There's a reason he is." She snorted in an elegant, ladylike way. "You've probably heard the rumors that my husband left me well provided for. I'm comfortable, but I'm certainly not as wealthy as the rumors suppose. I miss my husband dearly, but thought after two years, maybe I should think about finding a nice man for the occasional outing. So when Victor asked me on a date, I thought, why not? But it was a big mistake."

"What happened?" Pru asked, intrigued.

"Ruff?"

"Aren't you a dear." Cynthia smiled down at Teddy. "The first date was at the café, where he paid. The second date was a walk in the park, which I thought was nice, although I was already thinking we didn't have much in common. Victor liked bragging about how many bargains he bought, and how he was able to haggle everyone down at garage sales and get everything he wanted for practically free!"

"That's not nice." Martha frowned. "And I like haggling – sometimes."

"The third date showed his true colors. He suggested we have dinner at Gary's Burger Diner."

"I love that place." Martha glanced at Pru. "We should go there again next week."

"Good idea," she replied, and then waited for the rest of the story.

"Well, I enjoyed my dinner, but as soon as the check arrived, Victor claimed he'd lost his wallet."

"Not that old trick." Martha groaned.

"Exactly." Cynthia nodded. "What could I do? I had to take him at his word, especially after he made a show of patting himself all over for his missing wallet. So I paid, and he promised he'd pay me back."

"I think we've all heard that," Martha said. "I bet you have too, Pru."

"Once," she replied, "but luckily it was only for a latte when I was in college."

"Smart girl." Martha nodded in approval.

"And then the next day, I bump into Victor at the supermarket register, *paying* for his groceries, and taking the cash out of his wallet!"

"Oh, no." Martha's mouth parted.

"So I said to him, 'I see you've found your wallet,' and he had the grace to flush the tiniest bit before making up some story about it falling out of his pocket in the car on the way to Gary's the previous night, and how he only found it down the side of the driver's seat when he got home."

"That's a good one," Martha commented.

"Isn't it?" Cynthia arched an eyebrow. "Maybe it's just as well he pulled that stunt on me, because it made me realize I'm not ready to dip my toe into the dating pool, especially with a man like him."

"I don't blame you," Pru murmured.

"I'm sure you'll be fine, dear," Cynthia said. "You probably have men lining up around the block to take you out."

"Not that you'd notice," Martha said cheerfully.

"Martha!" Pru's cheeks felt hot.

"But there is a Detective Hottie on the scene – somewhere."

"Really?" Cynthia looked interested.

"It's nothing," Pru said quickly, not wanting to discuss her love life – or lack of one – right now. Especially with someone she'd just met.

"His name's Jesse," Martha continued, "and he's Mitch's friend. And now Mitch has hired him as a detective."

"I'm so glad Detective Castern retired," Cynthia said. "I did not like that man."

"He was yucky," Martha agreed. "Hopefully Jesse is much better than him."

"Yes, indeed," Cynthia replied. After browsing Martha's items, she finally settled on a dessert cookbook, and gave Martha a dollar.

"Thanks." Martha grinned, tucking the cash into the pouch slung around her waist.

More customers drifted over, and before long Martha had sold some of her old clothes and more cookbooks, but no one had been tempted by her holey socks.

"What's the time?" she asked Pru.

Pru obliged by looking at her watch. "Ten-thirty."

"Is that all? I feel like I've been here for hours."

"I know what you mean." Pru relaxed in the plastic chair, which was surprisingly comfortable. "Would you like to take a look around while I man the stall?"

"Good idea." Martha whipped off the pouch and handed it to her, then rose, gripping the handles of her rolling walker.

"I'll mind Teddy if you like," she offered.

"Yeah, I don't want him getting tangled up in the wheels," Martha admitted. Looking down at the white fluffball, she said, "You be good for Pru, now. When I get back, you two could take a stroll around."

"Ruff!" Teddy wagged his tail so hard, Pru wondered if it would fall off.

Holding Teddy's lead, she scanned the crowd for potential customers, but no one looked like they were tempted by their table.

It was pleasant sitting in the winter sunshine, and after a few minutes, her eyelids drooped. She blinked rapidly, suddenly aware of a large shadow in front of her. Opening her eyes, she drew in her breath at the man standing before her. Around thirty, with short, wavy dark hair and a rugged, attractive face, she didn't want to admit to herself that she found him appealing.

"What are you doing here, Jesse?" she blurted.

"Ruff!" *Hi!*

"Just taking a look around." He picked up a pair of holey red socks. "These yours?"

"No."

"Didn't think so. How's the senior sleuthing club? Got a new case?"

"Not at the moment," she said, wondering why she got hot and bothered in his presence, even when he wore faded jeans and a gray sweatshirt. "But," she suddenly remembered the argument between Victor and Peggy, "a man was burgled last month and his blue shepherdess statue was stolen."

"How do you know that?" His gaze sharpened.

"I heard him telling practically everyone about it this morning." She gestured to the neighboring table. "He accused his neighbor of stealing it, but she was able to provide proof that she owned her similar looking statue."

"You're not talking about Victor, are you?"

"Yes."

"We're still working on that investigation. I interviewed the neighbors and they were all out, either at work or doing errands. No one saw anything and no one knows anything about it."

"So it happened during the day?"

"Yes."

"You're not here because you're hoping to find the stolen statue?"

"No." He shook his head. "It's my day off. And I doubt that someone would try to sell a valuable antique – if it is one – for a few dollars at a church garage sale – although stranger things can happen." He paused. "Maybe it's a case for the senior sleuthing club." There was a grin in his eyes.

"What are you saying about my club?" Martha barreled up to him, looking flushed.

"I mentioned to Pru that maybe you should look into that stolen shepherdess statue – but I was joking," he ended hastily when Martha's expression brightened. "Leave it to us."

"You haven't found it yet," Martha retorted.

"I'm sure we will," he replied.

"Pooh – you sound just like Mitch." Martha wheeled the walker around to the opposite side of the table and sat down. Eyeing the pair of socks in his hand, she said, "Wanna buy them?"

"Thanks, but I don't have a need for them. I was just browsing." He placed the socks back on the table.

"You could make a toy for Teddy with them," Martha suggested.

Pru hid a smile as Teddy eagerly said, "Ruff!"

"I'm sure he has plenty of toys already," Jesse said good-naturedly.

"He does," Pru confirmed.

Jesse checked his watch. "I'd better be going. See you around."

"Well, pooh," Martha muttered after he departed. "And you're not wearing your lipstick."

"I thought we'd decided I didn't need to wear it if I didn't want to," she replied, suddenly feeling a lot younger than her mid-twenties.

"Yeah, I guess," Martha agreed. "Oh, well. I'm sure he'll come back. Ooh – look! There's Victor."

"Where?" Pru squinted but couldn't see the man who had accused Peggy of stealing his shepherdess.

"Over there." Martha nudged her. "Oh, no – he's coming over here!"

Her eyes widened as Martha's prediction came true. But just as he picked up a casserole cookbook, another man around the same age came up to him, wearing old jeans and a khaki sweater.

"It's me, Brian," the second man said. "From Oregon. I recognized you right away."

Victor turned around slowly, his expression registering surprise. "Brian." His mouth parted, and he squinted at the man. "Yes, it is you! I didn't recognize you with your gray hair. How are you?"

"I saw you the other day in the bank," Brian said. "I was sure it was you, but you didn't seem to see me."

"I'm sorry." Victor shook his head. "I must have been focusing on my deposit and didn't notice you. When I'm concentrating, I'm not aware of anything else."

"I think I look exactly the same," Brian said, "apart from gray hair and a few wrinkles." He tapped the crow's feet around his eyes.

Observing the exchange, Pru had to admit that Brian did look pretty good for his age – somewhere in his sixties? He was a little tanned, with a wide forehead and strong chin.

"But you look a little different." Brian looked at him appraisingly. "I'm not sure what it is – maybe your hair – you've lost a bit."

Victor smoothed his thinning gray hair back from his widow's peak. "These things happen." He eyed Brian's full head of hair enviously. "But apparently not to you."

"Not yet." Brian shrugged.

"So, what are you doing in Gold Leaf Valley?" Victor asked.

"I've just moved here. Houses are cheaper here and now I've retired, I don't need to live in a city anymore. How about you? I would have thought somewhere like this would be the last place you would live. You loved going out on the town when we hung out together in Portland."

"I like it here," Victor told him. "It suits me. And I go out plenty. When I want."

"Are you married?"

"No, but I'm seeing a nice widow."

Pru and Martha glanced at each other.

"How about grabbing a cup of coffee at that cat cafe?" Brian suggested. "We can catch up on old times."

"Sure thing. It's good to see you." Victor stepped away from the table, clutching the cookbook.

"Hold your horses," Martha commanded. "Are you going to buy that book or not?"

"This?" Victor glanced down at the casserole cookbook in his hand. "Oh, yeah."

"How much is it?" Brian asked.

"One dollar," Martha replied.

"You can afford that, can't you?" Brian turned to his friend.

"Of course I can." Victor dug into his trousers' pocket and hunted for the cash. "Here you go." He held out a crumpled one-dollar bill.

Pru took it, so Martha wouldn't have to get up. "Thanks."

Victor nodded and walked away, talking to his long-lost friend.

"Huh," Martha said. "Cynthia said she wasn't dating him anymore."

"Unless he's found another nice widow," Pru suggested.

Martha's eyes widened. "I've gotta find out! I'll go to the senior center on Monday and get the gossip!"

"Ruff?" Teddy looked up at her.

"I know you wanna come with me," Martha said, "but the senior center is being poopy about allowing dogs in. I'll have to find out about making you an emotional support dog and then you can visit everywhere with me."

"Ruff!" *Yes!*

A distant rumble and chug chug sounded. Pru looked over at the parking lot. A minibus pulled up, and moments later, seniors started carefully descending.

"More customers!" Martha's eyes lit up.

"How much have you made so far?"

"Eight dollars," Martha replied, unzipping her pouch and rifling through the bills and coins. "I've made a profit already!"

"Ruff!" Teddy's tail wagged.

"It's Mrs. Finch." Pru waved to the elderly lady who tapped her way over on the grass. Her beige skirt and dusty rose cardigan looked very suitable for the weather.

"Hi, Mrs. Finch," Martha greeted her. "Want a cookbook? On the house." She waved her hand over the several remaining books.

"That's very kind of you." Mrs. Finch smiled at them, her gaze drifting down through her delicate pink spectacles to where Teddy stood. "Hello, Teddy."

"Ruff!" *Hello!*

"He's being such a good boy," Martha said proudly.

"I can see." Mrs. Finch's eyes twinkled. "I think it's wonderful Father Mike has organized all this." She gestured to the neighboring tables displaying their items and the small crowds gathered here and there.

"There's even a donation bucket at the church gate."

"I didn't see it when we arrived," Pru said.

"Maybe Father Mike put it out after," Martha suggested.

"It might have been Zoe's idea," Mrs. Finch added. "She was talking about it last night at craft club."

"That Zoe." Martha chuckled affectionately. "She has some good ideas."

"How is your retired lady detective script coming along?" Mrs. Finch asked.

"Not too well." Martha pouted. "I haven't worked on it much lately." Her gaze landed on Teddy, and her eyes widened. "But she could adopt a dog just like Teddy! And he helps her solve the case. Wouldn't it be something if it did get made into a TV show? Teddy could star in it!"

"Ruff!" *Yes!* Teddy swiveled around in a circle, looking excited.

"What about you?" Pru asked mischievously. "You could play the retired lady detective."

"Ha!" Martha hooted. "I'd love to. I can just see me and Teddy in Hollywood, hobnobbing with all the big shots, having lunch at posh restaurants, driving down the palm tree lined streets – just like in those TV shows. But I'm not an actress."

"Maybe you could take a crash course," Pru suggested.

"Good one! I bet that would be so fun! But I'd have to play my lady detective wheeling a walker around." Martha patted the handle of her rolling walker. "This does a good job of getting me places."

"Ruff," Teddy agreed.

They chatted for a few more minutes with Mrs. Finch, and then she left to browse the other tables, declining Martha's offer of a cookbook, saying she had too many already, and perhaps she should have her own garage sale one day.

"Things are quiet now," Martha said. "Wanna take a walk around with Teddy? I can manage."

"If you're sure?" Pru looked at the twos and threes of people drifting past, but no one stopping at the table.

"Ruff!" Teddy nudged Pru's leg.

"Ooh – maybe he's gotta do his business somewhere." Martha suddenly looked panicked. "I didn't bring any poop bags with me."

"I did." Pru patted her small purse hanging over her shoulder. "I've got one in there."

"Oh, good." Martha sounded relieved. "You'd better take him, then. Maybe around the back of the church, so he's not distracted and can concentrate on doing it."

"Ruff!" Teddy agreed, walking by Pru's side as they left the busy front garden and walked around to the rear of the church hall.

"How about here?" Pru gestured to the deserted green lawn – they were the only people around.

After sniffing the grass, Teddy got comfy and did his business, which Pru picked up with the plastic baggie.

"Hopefully there's a trash can somewhere," she murmured, glancing around, but not seeing one.

She and Teddy strolled around the small back garden, finding a trash can on the way, and she smiled down at him. "Want to check out the other tables?"

"Ruff!" *Yes!*

They rounded the side of the church and headed toward a table that was piled with all sorts of items, including books and clothes. Pru was tempted to buy an old mystery novel, when raised voices caught her attention.

"No, I don't think so," a woman's voice said.

Pru frowned. It sounded like Cynthia.

"But why not?"

Pru turned her head, her eyes widening when she spied Victor and Cynthia standing next to an oak tree, a short distance away from the tables.

Victor's voice was loud, and she wasn't the only person watching the couple.

"What's going on?" Doris asked, her face a little flushed. Her table was nearby and looked like plenty of customers had rummaged through her goods, untidy piles of clothes littered everywhere.

"I didn't see you," Pru apologized. She tilted her head toward the oak tree.

"Oh, Victor. He's not a nice man." Doris frowned. "I heard what happened with him and Cynthia at Gary's that night when he forgot to pay. I was working in the kitchen, and Cindy, the waitress, told me all about it later. Apparently Cynthia was embarrassed about the whole thing, and I don't blame her! But Cindy said Victor was as cool as an ice cube about the whole thing and didn't seem embarrassed at all."

"We had a good time, didn't we?" Victor attempted a wheedling tone in his voice but couldn't quite achieve it.

"You might have," Cynthia said. She shook her head. "I've realized I'm not ready to date again. And when I do, I'll go out with a man who treats me right and isn't a cheapskate." She strode off, her head high, and her shoulders back. Pru silently applauded her.

"Is that your nice widow?" Victor's friend Brian came up to him, holding a straw hat. "Sorry about that."

"It's nothing." Victor brushed off the scene. "She'll come to her senses. And if she doesn't, there are plenty of other women out there."

"If you say so." Brian didn't sound convinced. "You're in your sixties now – and you haven't walked down the aisle yet."

"Not everyone needs to get married," Victor replied brusquely. "I've finished looking around. I might as well go home. No one wanted to haggle with me." He held up his empty hands.

"Too bad," Brian said. "This hat will be great to keep the sun off me when I'm gardening in summer."

"I looked at that," Victor grumbled. "She wouldn't budge and wanted five dollars for it."

"I got it for four." Brian grinned.

Victor muttered something and shook his head. "Well, see you around."

"Why don't we meet at the café next week for coffee?" Brian suggested.

Victor looked tempted for a moment, then shook his head. "Nah. It's too expensive. I could make myself ten cups of coffee at home for what they charge. And I don't like cats."

"I think the cat could tell," Brian replied. "Why don't we meet there and you can bring your own coffee with you? They probably wouldn't mind, since you sent your coffee back twice this morning before you were satisfied with it."

Pru and Doris stared at each other.

"He sent his coffee back?" Doris mouthed, her expression one of shock.

"Twice?" Pru mimed.

"It wasn't hot enough the first time," Victor protested, "and the second time they didn't give me a peacock on the latte art. I've heard all about how that girl Lauren can do this great artwork. And all she gave me was a swan." He shook his head in disgust. "She should automatically give every customer a peacock. She'll never get out of this town if she doesn't give customers what they want one hundred percent of the time."

"She's not a mind reader," Brian said mildly.

"Well, she should be," Victor snapped. "If you really want to meet again, let's hang out at the park and bring our own beverages. What about Monday morning?"

"Okay." Brian nodded. "See you then."

Victor walked away.

"Wow," Doris's tone was one of disbelief. "I can't believe that guy. I think Cynthia was lucky to discover what he was like so soon."

"I know what you mean."

"Ruff!" Teddy's button brown eyes were wide as he stared after Victor.

Brian browsed another table, and then moved off.

"And I thought the most exciting thing that happened this morning was selling my old sweater for three dollars!"

"Have you made many sales?" Pru asked.

"A few. Some of the kids were enthusiastic about going through everything – and some of their parents were, too." Doris started shaking out the remaining clothes – tops in muted colors, and some denim jeans – and refolding them.

"I'd better get back to Martha."

"I bet she'll want to hear about that conversation Victor and his friend just had."

"Definitely."

CHAPTER 4

Martha's eyes rounded when Pru told her about the conversation she'd witnessed – first with Victor and Cynthia, and then Victor and Brian.

"Victor's a real grumpy pants – and a miser," Martha commented. "Did you see the way he tried to steal my cookbook?"

"Maybe he forgot he held it because he was talking to his friend Brian." Pru tried to be fair, but it was a little difficult. "If you hadn't said something, I would have."

"I know you would." Martha nodded. "And I bet Teddy would have told him to pay for it, too."

"Ruff!"

"Have you sold anything else?" Pru thought the table looked a little emptier.

"Someone bought a pair of holey socks." Martha chuckled. "I'd given up on selling any of them. And they were the ones with the red argyle pattern."

"I wonder what they'll do with them."

"Maybe darn them and wear them," Martha said. "I'm not too good with the sewing. But maybe I should keep going with it, and make Teddy some more bandanas to wear. He looks so cute and smart wearing that one." She pointed to his scarlet bandana around his neck.

"Ruff!" *Yes!*

"Who wants some cupcakes?" Zoe appeared, waving a cardboard box.

"Me!" Martha's face lit up. "Goody!"

"We decided to close early." Lauren appeared next to Zoe, with Annie on her leash. "Nearly all our customers are over here this morning."

"Ruff." Teddy tugged on his lead, wanting to be closer to his friend.

Pru obliged and the two fur babies said hello to each other by gently patting each other on the shoulder again.

"Did you get two men coming in for coffee this morning?" Pru asked.

"Yeah." Zoe made a face. "One was okay, but the other was this real grump who sent back Lauren's latte twice." She sounded outraged. "Nobody does that!"

"First he complained it wasn't hot enough, and then when I remade it, grumbled that he only got a swan and not a peacock." Lauren sighed. "The peacock is the most complicated design we do, and I thought he might not want to wait too long."

"I think he might complain about a lot of things." Pru tried to cheer her up.

"You'd better watch it if he comes back to the café – he might try to steal something!" Martha put in.

"Really?" Zoe's eyes widened.

"Martha—" Pru attempted, but her roommate told them all about Victor nearly walking off with one of her cookbooks.

"And then he pulled a fast one on Cynthia." Martha proceeded to tell them all about Cynthia's date with Victor at Gary's Burger Diner.

"Martha," Pru tried again, "maybe Cynthia doesn't want everyone to know about that."

"Oops." Martha looked contrite. "Yeah. Sorry. But I know you girls won't tell anyone. Will you?"

"Nope." Zoe zipped her lips shut and locked them.

"You know I won't," Lauren put in.

"Yeah. You're a good girl." Martha beamed at her.

"What about me?" Zoe looked mock-outraged.

"You're a good girl, too." Martha chuckled. "So is Pru. With all you good girls around, you make me want to be good, too."

They all laughed, Teddy adding a happy ruff, although Pru wondered if he really knew what they were talking about this time.

Annie, though, seemed to know exactly what they were saying, and Pru wondered if she had imagined the slight nod the Norwegian Forest Cat gave at Martha's statement.

Lauren and Zoe said they were going to browse the tables, Lauren declining Martha's offer of a free cookbook.

"I have so many at home," she apologized. "Zoe, what about you?"

"Let me see." Zoe flicked through a couple. "Do you have any for air fryers?"

"No. These are old." Martha tapped a Thai recipe book. "Before air fryers were invented. And my doctor says I shouldn't eat spicy things at my age." She pouted. "And sometimes I think he might be right. Pooh."

"This looks good." Zoe pointed to a chicken dish in the Thai book. "But I have to buy all these spices. Ooh – maybe Chris would like this book. He makes the best chili and uses spices."

"He does." Lauren nodded.

"Brrt," Annie added.

"I'll get him this." Zoe dug out her wallet from her jeans' pocket. "It will be a nice surprise for him when he gets home from his shift tonight."

"How's the paramedic crew doing now?" Martha asked.

"It's good, since they hired that nice guy a while ago." Zoe smiled. "Chris loves his job, and now everyone working there gets along with each other, he loves it even more."

"I'm glad," Pru said.

"Yeah, Chris had a horrid guy working with him a while ago – until he got murdered," Martha said.

"Not by Chris," Zoe rushed to assure her.

"Chris wouldn't hurt anyone," Lauren added.

"Brrt." *No.*

"Put your money away," Martha told Zoe.

"I insist." Zoe pressed two dollars in her hand. "Is that enough? I can give you more." She flicked through the bills in her wallet.

"More than enough," Martha said gruffly.

"This way I can tell Chris I bought him something," Zoe explained.

"Was it your idea to put the donation bucket at the church gates?" Pru asked, remembering what someone had said earlier that morning.

"Yes." Zoe grinned. "I ran into Father Mike after I took your cupcake order and said it would encourage people to make a donation. I shook the bucket when we came back just now and it jingled away with coins."

"Goody." Martha beamed. "I don't like to think of people going hungry because they can't afford to buy enough food to eat."

"Neither do I," Lauren replied somberly. "I put some money in the bucket just now."

"And Pru here gave Father Mike some cash when we arrived." Martha gave her an approving look. "With all you good girls around, I'm gonna have to step up!"

***

People started packing up their unsold items just before one o'clock.

"What am I going to do with this stuff?" Martha waved a hand over her table. She hadn't sold any more holey socks, and still had three cookbooks and an old pair of sweatpants.

"I think you've done well," Pru encouraged.

"At least I made twelve dollars profit." Martha cheered up. "That's enough to buy Teddy some treats."

Hearing that special word, Teddy looked up from sniffing the grass, a hopeful expression on his face.

"Here." Martha reached into her pocket and gave him a dog cookie. "I've been saving it all morning for you."

"Ruff!" *Thank you.* He wolfed it down and looked at her expectantly for more.

"Just one this time, little guy," Martha said indulgently.

"Would you like a drink?" Pru grabbed his travel bowl and filled it from a water bottle she'd packed for him. Pouring it into the bowl, she put it down on the grass.

The sound of Teddy's tongue lapping the water made her smile.

"Thanks," Martha said. "I guess I can ask Father Mike if he would like to have this stuff."

"Good idea."

Pru packed the remaining items in one of the boxes they'd brought with them that morning. Her stomach rumbled.

"Let's go home and get some lunch," Martha said. "And eat those yummy cupcakes as well."

"You're on." She finished packing the box.

"Are you leaving now?" Father Mike materialized, and checked his notebook.

"Would you like the stuff in the box?" Martha asked. "It's some cookbooks and old clothes."

"Are you sure you don't want to keep them?" he asked.

"Nope." Martha shook her head. "They're all yours." She hesitated. "There are some holey socks in there. I can keep them if you don't want them?"

"I'm sure I can find something to do with them, or one of my parishioners could use them for crafts, I imagine."

Pru handed him the box. "It's not heavy."

"Thanks."

Father Mike walked over to the next table, and they got ready to leave.

"Ruff?" Teddy looked hopefully at Martha.

"Uh oh. I know that look. I think he needs to do his business again," Martha said.

"Last time we went behind the church and I picked it up," Pru said. "We could go there again?"

"Yeah, and give him some privacy." Martha nodded. "Come on little guy, you can go in a minute."

Pru held his lead while Martha trundled along with her walker. Martha waved to a fluffy white cat peering out of the parsonage window. "Hi, Mrs. Snuggle!" she called, and then they rounded the church. Pru gestured to the green lawn at the back of the hall.

"Ruff!" Teddy forgot about what he was there to do and charged forward.

"What …" Pru's voice tailed off as she stared at Victor lying on the grass.

CHAPTER 5

"Is he dead?" Martha raced forward with her walker.

"Maybe we shouldn't get too close," Pru warned.

"You're right, we don't want to disturb the crime scene."

"Ruff!" Teddy strained against his harness.

"There's a knife," Martha observed, pointing to the blood-stained implement on the ground next to Victor.

"And it looks like he's been stabbed in the chest." Pru shuddered.

Victor had his eyes closed, a look of surprise on his face.

"We'd better call Mitch." Martha referred to Lauren's husband, who was the head detective in the small town. She took her phone out of her walker basket and dialed.

"He said to stay here and not touch anything," Martha said a minute later. "He'll be right over."

Teddy jiggled around on the grass.

"Why don't I take him over there?" Pru pointed a short distance away.

"Good idea. You go and do your business, little guy."

After Pru used another poo bag she luckily had in her purse, they returned to Martha. Out of the corner of her eye, she saw lights flash at the front side of the church.

Mitch and Jesse rounded the corner, followed by two paramedics.

"Hi, Chris," Martha called. "The dead body is over there." She pointed to where Victor lay.

Pru nodded to Chris. She'd met him once at the café and he seemed to be a nice guy.

"How did you find him?" Mitch asked. Wearing dark slacks and a white button-down shirt, he looked calm and capable. His short dark hair, serious brown eyes, and firm chin added to that impression. Jesse accompanied him.

Martha explained how Teddy needed to go to the bathroom.

"And that's when we saw him, right, Pru?"

"That's right," she hastily replied, trying not to look at Jesse.

"It's Victor," Jesse said. "The man who reported a stolen statue last month."

"I know him." Mitch nodded. "I thought he looked familiar."

"And apparently today he got into an argument with his neighbor, accusing her of stealing his blue shepherdess statue," Jesse remarked.

"Ruff!" Teddy agreed, first sniffing Jesse's shoes, and then Mitch's.

"Then he met a friend here," Martha remembered. "At my table. He nearly walked off with one of my cookbooks, he was so involved with talking to his pal."

"Do you know who he was?" Mitch asked.

"Brian," Pru answered. "That's what Victor called him. They went to the café, and then came back here for more browsing, and planned to meet up at the park on Monday."

"How do you know all this?" Jesse frowned.

"I overheard them talking near one of the tables when Teddy and I stretched our legs."

"Anyone else he had problems with this morning?" Mitch asked. "Jesse, you were here."

"I didn't see anything out of the ordinary," Jesse replied. "I was having a relaxing morning. For once." He looked at Mitch ruefully. "I know it's part of the job."

"Unfortunately." Mitch nodded.

"Cynthia," Pru blurted.

"Who?" Jesse frowned.

"The nice widow Victor was dating." Martha told them all about how Victor forgot his wallet at the restaurant.

"That's low." Jesse shook his head. "A decent guy wouldn't do that."

"No, he wouldn't," Mitch confirmed.

"I take it you're talking about yourself, Jesse?" Martha quizzed. "I know Mitch wouldn't do something like that."

"Neither would I," Jesse confirmed, glancing sideways at Pru.

Chris and his colleague carried Victor away on a stretcher.

"We'll have to wait for the ME's official report," Mitch said, "but it looks like murder to me."

***

After Mitch finished questioning them, they were free to go home.

"Goody," Martha said as they walked back to the car. "I'm sorry Victor is dead, but he wasn't a nice man."

"He didn't seem nice this morning," Pru agreed.

"Ruff!"

"At least we found out something," Martha continued.

"What's that?"

"Detective Hottie won't sneak out of a restaurant without paying." She glanced at Pru, who walked beside her. "He doesn't seem to care that you're not wearing lipstick, either. That's good."

"Plenty of women don't wear makeup these days," Pru felt obliged to defend herself. "It wears off anyway, even the ones that are guaranteed to stay on longer." At least, that had been her experience. "Or else it dries my lips out. And I usually wear a plain lip balm with SPF to protect them from the sun." She glanced up at the winter sky – the sun crowding out the small gray clouds.

"That's good." Martha nodded. "You gotta protect yourself. Okay. Hmm. Maybe you and Detective Hottie are into the same hobbies and you don't even know it."

"Like reading? I haven't seen him come into the library."

"Maybe he's got one of those e-readers and buys all his books online and reads them on that. When I'm at the café next week, I'll ask Lauren and Zoe if they know anything about him, apart from being Mitch's friend."

"What he does in his spare time really doesn't concern me." But Pru wondered if she was trying to convince herself, as well as Martha.

***

"It's time for the next meeting of the senior sleuthing club," Martha announced that afternoon. They'd just finished their lunch, the cupcakes adding a welcome note to the dessert portion of the meal, and they were relaxing in the living room, Teddy sitting on the sofa next to Martha.

"What for?" Pru's eyes widened. "You don't mean we should investigate Victor's death?"

"You betcha! We were right there, on the scene – again. Plus we gave Mitch and Jesse valuable info. I know Cynthia and Peggy, too. I bet they don't."

"We don't know anything about Victor's friend, Brian," Pru said.

"Maybe I can find out at the senior center on Monday," Martha replied, "and if Victor was seeing another nice widow besides Cynthia, or if it was just talk to impress his friend this morning."

"But anyone could have killed Victor. There were plenty of people in

the church grounds this morning.
Maybe he had more than one
enemy."

"Good point." Martha looked
thoughtful.

"Ruff!"

"I guess we could talk to Peggy,"
Pru said a little reluctantly.

"His neighbor – good thinking."
Martha nodded. "And I know where
she lives, so we can visit her next
week. Maybe she saw something
about this burglar without realizing it. I
wonder how long ago it was?"

"Victor said last month, during his
argument with her this morning," Pru
suddenly remembered.

"See? You're good at this, too."
Martha beamed approval at her.

"Ruff!" Teddy agreed.

"Thanks. But I still think we should
leave this to the police."

"But don't you want to solve this
before Detective Hottie can? He
doesn't seem to think the senior
sleuthing club is much chop – but we
can show him who is the fastest
sleuth."

"That would be nice." She was tempted. "But it is his job – and Mitch's."

"I bet they've got other cases as well." Martha waved a hand. "Like finding out who stole Victor's blue shepherdess statue. They still haven't solved that."

"Maybe talking to Peggy will turn up something."

"Ruff!"

CHAPTER 6

Pru spent a pleasant Sunday reading a mystery novel borrowed from the library. Martha puttered around the house, and tried to sew a new bandana for Teddy, although it didn't turn out quite the way she expected.

"Two corners are a bit wonky," she complained to Pru that evening, holding up the scarlet fabric. "I need some different material as well – I want Teddy to have all sorts of colors!"

"Ruff!" Teddy lifted a paw to pat at the square of cloth.

"I'm sure no one will be able to tell it's a bit crooked when Teddy is wearing it."

"Let's see." Martha bent down and tied it gently around his neck. "What do you think, little guy?"

"What if he stands in front of a mirror?"

"Yes!" Martha brightened. "I bet he would love that. There's one on the bathroom door."

They headed into the bathroom, Pru closing the door behind them.

"What do you think, Teddy?" Pru bent down, appearing in the mirror's reflection with the white fluffball.

"Ruff!" Teddy preened a little, his brown eyes wide as he stared at himself.

"I think he knows he's looking at himself and not another dog," Martha said. "Do you like your new bandana?"

"Ruff!" *Yes!*

"And I can't see any wonky corners," Pru commented.

"No, it looks good after all." Martha admired her handiwork. "And only a little bit rumpled."

"I don't think Teddy minds." She smiled at the dog through the mirror and he seemed to smile back.

"Goody. Maybe next week I can buy some more fabric. There's a small craft shop I can go to."

They finished the evening by watching a spy drama. Teddy fell asleep on the sofa soon after the movie started.

"It must be all that playing in the yard this afternoon," Martha said.

They'd both taken Teddy out to romp around with his ball a few hours earlier, Martha sitting on her walker and throwing it for him, then Pru took over.

"I think it's tired me out, too." Pru covered a yawn. But it had been fun.

***

The next day, Pru's boss Barbara was not in a good mood.

"Shelve these books as quickly as you can," she said brusquely, the severe edges of her dark bob hitting her cheeks. "We have three groups coming in today and I need you to set up the spaces for them. Greek conversation, then Spanish, and an art group." She shuddered. "They've assured me they'll only be using pencils. I told the group leader I do not want paint being splashed around in my library."

Barbara was the head librarian and could be strict, but Pru was grateful she had this job. She still had student loans to pay, and an incident at college had seemed to make her unhirable – until she'd accepted the position here as assistant librarian.

"Yes, Barbara." She wheeled the trolley full of books to the As and started neatly putting the books back into place, exactly where they belonged.

When she was finished, she set up the small room next door – a large, horseshoe shaped table with hard plastic chairs, and a screen adorning one wall.

And just in time. She recognized some of the members of the new Greek conversation group – apparently they were friends who'd decided to cruise the Greek Isles together, and wanted to learn some of the language.

After scanning some of the recent returns and piling them on the now cleared trolley, she looked up, her eyes widening when Jesse strode into the quiet space.

"What are you doing here?" she couldn't help saying.

"I thought I'd see if you had any of the latest thrillers," he replied. "I'm on my lunchbreak."

"Is it that time already?" Glancing at her watch, she noted it was almost her lunch hour. She'd been so absorbed in her tasks – one of the things she loved about her job – she hadn't even realized.

"Yeah." He smiled.

"The new thrillers are over here." She rounded the counter and led him to a small display nearby. "I'm sorry there aren't any more this month. If there's one you'd like that we don't have, you could put in a request and the library might buy it." Was she babbling? She hoped not.

"You've got it." He plucked a thick hardback with a man's silhouette on the cover. "Thanks."

"You're welcome." She headed back to the counter.

A minute later, he stood in front of her again. "Can you check me out?"

"Of course." She glanced discreetly at the self-checkout machine in the corner. No one was using it. After scanning his card, she checked out the book and tucked the receipt inside. "There you go."

"Thanks."

"How are you going with the case?" she heard herself asking.

"We've finished interviewing everyone at the garage sale who was there when we arrived. No one saw or heard anything. Apparently. But don't worry. We'll crack the case."

"What about Victor's meeting with Brian today at the park?"

"A guy named Brian was there this morning. We staked it out. He said he hadn't heard his friend was dead, and we hadn't interviewed him on Saturday after you found Victor's body, so he must have left the garage sale by then. Apparently he doesn't watch the news much or buy the local newspaper."

When Pru didn't comment, he continued, "I hope you and the senior sleuthing club don't interfere. Mitch and I have got this."

"Their names are Martha and Teddy," she reminded him. "And you can't stop Martha going to the senior center like she usually does."

"I doubt she'll find out anything useful there. Apart from how to sneak Teddy in with her."

Pru stared at him. How did he know Martha had thought of that idea, before reluctantly discarding it last night?

***

"Guess what I found out today!" Martha greeted her when she walked through the front door late afternoon.

"What?" She bent down to stroke Teddy, who'd run up to her, his tail wagging happily.

"Victor was only seeing Cynthia," Martha replied. "So when he told Brian on Saturday he was seeing a nice widow, he was lying. Because

Cynthia told us she was done with him."

"That's right." She sank down onto the sofa, and helped Teddy up. He snuggled into her lap.

"We had playtime in the yard this afternoon," Martha said. "He wanted to go out to do you know what, and I thought it was a good opportunity to let him have a bit of a runaround. But maybe we overdid it. It's easy for me to sit on the walker and throw the ball for him. He brings it right back to me!"

"I'm sure it's good for him to romp around and tire himself out a little at times," Pru said.

"I hope so." Martha peered at her fur baby. "Sorry if we had too much fun, little guy."

Teddy mumbled something sleepily, and burrowed his head further into Pru's lap.

"So Victor wanted to impress his friend Brian by saying he was still seeing Cynthia," Pru said in a low voice, so as not to wake up Teddy.

"It looks like it," Martha agreed. "So we know something else about Victor

– he was a liar. Now we have to find out about Brian and Peggy."

"Apparently Brian didn't know Victor was killed." She briefly explained about Jesse's appearance at the library that day.

"Huh." Martha frowned. "I don't know why this Brian guy wants to be friends with Victor again – although he's dead now. He was a real grump – and a miser. But," she brightened, "it looks like you and Jesse do have something in common – books!"

"I haven't read many thrillers," Pru replied, but she'd already been intrigued by the book Jesse had borrowed. But … would he enjoy the cozy mysteries she sometimes read?

"Tomorrow," Martha said, "I'll go to the café and see if they know anything about Detective Hottie apart from being Mitch's friend."

"You don't have to do that," she replied hastily.

"Maybe I want to know as well." Martha pouted. "He doesn't think much of my – our – sleuthing club. And then we can make a date to visit

Peggy. What time do you get off work this week?"

"Tomorrow is four, the same as today," Pru answered. "Wednesday is five, and Thursday is four again."

"We'll have to make it tomorrow, I guess," Martha said. "Is that okay with you? We can go to Peggy's as soon as you come home. She only lives a few blocks away and we can take your car. And," she added, "I bet we'll be hungry after that. We could have dinner at Gary's Burger Diner on the way home." She looked hopefully at Pru.

"That sounds like a great idea." She loved Gary's burgers even though she'd only been here a few months.

"Goody." Martha beamed.

"What about Teddy?" She gently stroked his white cottony fur as he lay sleeping on her lap. "I don't think we can take him to Gary's."

"Pooh. Because I bet Peggy would love to meet him." Martha sighed. "I guess we'll have to leave him here for a little while."

"Maybe you should look into seeing if you can get him certified as an emotional support dog, and then you can take him everywhere."

"Yeah, I was going to." Martha nodded. "He's only ten months old, though. I'd better check if they have a minimum age."

They discussed what to have for dinner that night. It was Pru's turn to cook and they agreed on chicken stir-fry.

"But make sure you cook the veggies soft enough," Martha directed. "I don't like veggies that are still practically raw."

"I understand." She didn't much like them that way herself.

By the time she served dinner, Teddy had woken up and sat with them at the small table in the kitchen after wolfing down his own dinner of meaty chunks in gravy.

"How about I bring back some cupcakes for us tomorrow?" Martha suggested at the end of the meal. "We can have them when we get home from Gary's tomorrow night."

"That sounds great." Her mouth watered at the thought.

***

The next day, her boss Barbara was in a better mood. The art group yesterday hadn't made a mess with their pencil drawings, and the conversation groups had run smoothly.

Today, there weren't any groups scheduled, and Barbara was ensconced at the reference desk, seemingly content to sort out a knotty problem including the different types of wood used to make furniture in the seventeen hundreds.

Pru couldn't help wondering throughout the day if Martha would glean any information about Jesse at the cafe, and then chided herself for the thought. She would be better to think up some questions to ask Peggy that afternoon, when they visited her.

Was Victor's stolen statuette the same as Peggy's blue shepherdess? Or was it really a valuable antique? Had Peggy been out of the house when the burglary took place? Had she noticed anything when she got back home?

By the time she arrived home, she was looking forward to talking to Peggy.

"I got the cupcakes!" Martha pointed to the kitchen. "I bought three, so we can have one and a half each. Lavender, triple chocolate ganache, and blueberry crumble."

"I can't wait." It was a shame they were saving them for dessert tonight and not tasting them right now.

"I know what you're thinking." Martha nodded and rose from the sofa, clutching the handles of the walker. "We should test them now – make sure they taste okay!"

"Are you a mind reader?" Pru joked, joining her and Teddy in the kitchen. The Coton looked up from his water dish, his expression curious.

"We're gonna have a little treat, and then go and visit Peggy," Martha explained to him. "And then stop off at Gary's later. Ooh – I know! Lauren buys Annie a plain meat patty from Gary's – maybe I could do the same for Teddy!"

"Ruff!" *Yes!* Teddy's tail wagged.

"Then that's what I'll do!"

They sat down at the kitchen table and tried the blueberry crumble cupcake, laden with a generous portion of berries.

"Delicious," Pru pronounced.

"Yeah, it's good." Martha nodded. "A hot chocolate with it would be even better, but I guess we don't have time. We should talk to Peggy before it gets too late – we don't want to interrupt her dinner."

After saying goodbye to Teddy and telling him they wouldn't be too long, they set off.

"Teddy's already had his meal," Martha told her, "so the Gary's patty will be supper for him."

"I'm sure he'll appreciate it."

"I hope so!"

Martha directed her to Peggy's house which was a few blocks away.

"I forgot to tell you what I found out about Jesse," Martha said when Pru parked outside a small Victorian house painted pale green. The front yard was neat and tidy with a few bushes here and there, and a tall tree with spindly branches hanging over the fence from the slightly ramshackle looking house next door.

"Oh?" She tried not to sound too interested.

"He's renting Mitch's old apartment. He was lucky to get it too, what with the housing situation here."

There hadn't been any rentals to be found when she'd arrived in Gold Leaf Valley last November.

"Lauren said it's pretty basic, but okay for a bachelor. Which is what Jesse is. He hangs out with Mitch and Chris, and Lauren and Zoe said they haven't heard a thing about a girlfriend."

"Mmm."

Martha chuckled. "Just thought I'd give you an update, that's all. If you ever want to know where his apartment is, just ask me – or Lauren and Zoe."

"Martha! Why would I want to know exactly where he lives?"

"You might want to deliver a book to him one day," Martha replied nonchalantly. "Home library service. Ha!" She grinned, then sobered. "Sorry." She patted Pru's shoulder. "Just tell me to back off if I'm being too pushy."

"Thanks." Pru smiled weakly at her.

"We'd better start sleuthing." Martha unbuckled her seatbelt.

Pru got the walker out of the trunk and then they made their way to Peggy's front door. The street was quiet and she checked her watch, surprised to see it was five-thirty already.

"I wonder what's going to happen to his house." Martha nodded to the gray house next door, with the tree overhanging Peggy's fence. "I bet that's Victor's."

"Wouldn't it go to his next of kin?"

"If he has any family," Martha replied. "He's a bachelor and I haven't heard of him having any relatives."

Pru knocked on Peggy's door.

After a moment, it opened, and Peggy, wearing warm pants and a yellow sweater, stared at them in surprise.

"Martha. What are you doing here?"

"Since me and Pru here found Victor, we thought we'd check around and find out a bit more about him," Martha said. "Have you met Pru? She's my roomie."

"You were at the garage sale." Peggy nodded. "When Victor accused me of stealing his blue shepherdess. I guess you'd better come in." Peggy headed down a short hallway, and turned right into a living room decorated in shades of sage and cream.

"Sit down," she invited, gesturing to a three-seater sofa, while she took the matching armchair.

Pru glanced around the neat and tidy room, her eyes widening a little as she spied the blue shepherdess statue standing proudly in a bookcase.

"I thought I'd display her properly after all the hoo-ha Victor made on Saturday." Peggy noticed her gaze. "I can't believe someone killed him – especially on church grounds – but well, it's not entirely unexpected."

"It's not?" Martha leaned forward eagerly.

"If you treat people the way he did, then you can expect a little payback eventually," Peggy explained. "Or a lot in his case."

"Who do you think killed him?" Martha asked.

"Everyone. Anyone." Peggy waved a hand. "Who knows? I know I put up with a lot living next door to him. You probably heard my rant at the garage sale. And you probably noticed those overhanging branches when you arrived. He just will not – would not – cut them down, even though I think he should. So I have to try and do it, and I've never been much of a gardener although I like to keep my yard neat."

"It is neat," Pru reassured her.

"Thanks." Peggy nodded. "I don't know what sort of information you're looking for. When my grandchildren came over to visit and accidentally threw a ball over the fence, he refused to give it back until I went over and demanded he return it. Little things like that, but over the years it adds up."

"We heard he was a bit of a miser," Martha said.

"Oh, yeah!" Peggy nodded. "He was always complaining about paying his property taxes, and then in the next breath bragging about this great deal he'd gotten. Do you know, he even had the nerve to tell me that I should cut my own hair at home instead of going to the salon? He said he cuts his own hair and doesn't understand how the barber has the nerve to charge so much!"

"I did notice his hair looked a little uneven," Pru remembered.

"Well, I'm certainly not going to try to cut my own hair," Peggy fumed. "I like it just the way it is, and Brooke does such a good job with it."

"She's the best." Martha patted her springy curls. "I love going to her. We have the best chats, too."

"So do we – I mean me and Brooke," Peggy replied. "She's such a nice girl – although I guess I should call her a lady, since I think she's about thirty now. That still seems like a girl to me." She sighed, and glanced at Pru. "You're just a girl to me, too, Pru. How I wish was your age again!"

"Me too." Martha nodded vigorously. "I guess the good thing about being older is we don't have to work anymore."

"There is that," Peggy agreed. "I retired two years ago from my job at a department store in Sacramento, and I don't miss the commute, that's for sure."

"Did Victor have any family?" Pru asked.

"Not that I know of," Peggy said after a moment. "I never saw any visitors arrive."

"What about him dating Cynthia?" Martha asked.

"I thought that was ridiculous!" Peggy snorted. "A man like him asking out a woman like Cynthia? I was surprised she agreed – but she soon came to her senses. I heard about how he 'forgot' his wallet when they went to Gary's Burger Diner. I think Cynthia spread it all over town and I don't blame her. If he tries – tried – to ask out anyone else, I think they would have heard about that incident and would have said no, if they had any sense."

"What about the burglary at his house?" Pru asked, her gaze straying to the blue shepherdess in the bookcase.

"The first I knew about that was when the police knocked on my door and asked if I'd heard or saw anything," Peggy said. "It happened last month. I was out shopping at the time."

"Did you notice anything out of the ordinary when you came home that day?" Pru asked.

Peggy thought for a moment. "No. I didn't see a smashed window or a door hanging open, or anything like that."

"Do you really think he had a statue like yours?" Martha stabbed her finger at the blue shepherdess. "Or was he making it up?"

Peggy's eyes widened and she sucked in a breath. "That would be just like him! And then claim it was a valuable antique and scam the insurance company!"

"Really?" Pru stared at her.

"Honey, you haven't lived next door to him. He would think it was a victimless crime and justify it to himself by saying the insurance companies make a lot of profit each year, so why shouldn't he get a piece of it?"

"What if," Martha said slowly, "he wasn't burgled at all? He just made it *all* up?"

"I wouldn't put it past him." Peggy nodded vigorously.

"And then he saw your blue shepherdess at the garage sale, and what? Decided to keep to the story about his being stolen, and try to claim yours?" Pru couldn't believe what she'd just said.

"See? I knew you'd be good at sleuthing," Martha told her approvingly.

"I think he would have enough nerve to do that," Peggy admitted. "Even if meant making a false statement to the police."

"We'll have to check with Mitch," Martha said after a moment. "Or Detective Hottie. See exactly what Victor claimed about this burglary."

"Maybe they'll know who inherits his estate," Pru said slowly.

"I don't know if he'd have much of one," Peggy snorted. "Apart from the house. And he didn't bother maintaining it like he should – he always complained that the repairs cost too much unless he did it himself."

"What did he do all day?" Pru asked.

"Apart from clipping coupons? I have no idea. He was free with his advice, but was pretty private about himself. I know he retired several years ago, but I have no idea what he did for a living. It might have been something very boring. I know I used to hear his car leave in the morning – even before I left for work, and saw him return around the same time as I did. I used to wave at him – just to be neighborly – and sometimes he'd nod before he went inside."

"What about pets?" Pru asked.

"No." Peggy shook his head. "I'm sure I'd know if he did. He'd probably say they were too expensive."

Martha tsked at that comment.

"But Teddy's worth it." Pru patted her hand.

"Where is he?' Peggy looked around the room, as if the little white dog would materialize any moment. "You didn't bring him."

"We're going to Gary's later and he's not allowed in there." Martha pouted. "But you're right, Pru, my life is so much better since I adopted Teddy, and again when you became my roomie."

"Ohhh. Mine too, Martha." And she meant it.

"Is there anything else I can help you with?" Peggy rose. "I have to start supper in a minute. I have to take my medication two hours after I finish eating, and I don't like to go to bed late."

"I hear you." Martha got up from the sofa and clutched the handles of her walker. "Pru?"

"I can't think of anything." She rose as well. "Thanks for talking to us."

"Anytime, dear." Peggy smiled. "As long as you bring your cute dog with you next time, Martha."

CHAPTER 7

When they arrived home from Gary's, both of them having enjoyed the smoky barbecue special with fries and a small chocolate shake, Pru wondered whether she had room for dessert. But when Martha showed her the lavender, and triple chocolate ganache cupcakes, she thought she could manage to fit them in.

"Ruff?" Teddy pranced around Pru's legs. The plain burger from Gary's filled the kitchen with its rich, savory aroma.

"We got you a cooked patty," Martha told him. "Just like Annie gets. It's got nothing in it but pure beef."

"Ruff!" *Yum!*

Martha crumbled it into his bowl and set it down for him. After testing it with his pink tongue, he dived into the morsel, making short work of his supper.

After licking the bowl clean, he looked up hopefully at Martha and Pru.

"Sorry, little guy, I only got you one. It's bedtime soon and you don't want to get indigestion."

Pru and Martha sat down at the table and dived into their cupcakes. Martha had cut them in half and gestured for Pru to choose her halves first. Each portion was pretty even.

"These are the best," Martha mumbled after her first mouthful.

"They are," she agreed around a mouthful of triple chocolate ganache. The chocolate cake crumb was studded with dark and white chocolate chips. The generous swirl of dark chocolate ganache on top was the finishing touch.

"Now we have to find out if Victor had a family and who he left his loot to," Martha continued.

"Loot?"

"You know, money, stocks and bonds, any other antiques." Martha chuckled. "And find out if Mitch thinks the burglary was fake or real."

"Jesse said they were investigating it," Pru said.

"But he's not gonna tell you if they have doubts about it, is he?" Martha wagged a finger. "Not yet, anyway, until you two know each other better. And then we have to talk to Cynthia and this Brian character," Martha continued. "We are gonna be busy, busy, busy!" She sounded delighted at the thought.

***

The next day, Pru had a few minutes of free time after shelving all the books and waiting for the French conversation group to arrive at the library. She'd already set things up for them, and Barbara had taken an early lunch.

She browsed online auction listings and found a couple of blue shepherdess statues that looked similar to Peggy's for sale for around fifty dollars. It appeared that Peggy had been correct and these types of statues had been mass produced a long time ago.

So did Victor's statue ever exist? Or was he hoping to make a something out of a nothing when he got burgled? If he really had been burgled, and hadn't faked the whole thing like Martha had suggested last night.

When she arrived home, Teddy eagerly greeted her at the door.

"Can you take him out to do his business?" Martha asked. She sat on the sofa, looking a little weary.

"Are you okay?" Martha was such a livewire that sometimes Pru forgot she was in her seventies, even though the rolling walker was a constant reminder.

"I'm fine." Martha waved away her concern. "I might have overdone it a little, that's all. I went to the senior center for gossip, and then I went to the café, and then I did a bit of grocery shopping."

"How did you bring the food home?"

"In my basket." Martha patted the back vinyl seat of her walker which hid a basket. "I only bought a few things, but all that walking tired me out a little."

"Can I make you a hot chocolate?"

"That would be great!" Martha brightened. "The mix isn't as good as the way Lauren makes it at the café, but it's not bad."

Pru made the hot chocolate first, promising herself she'd enjoy one after she took Teddy out to the yard.

After throwing the ball a few times for him, she looked around the small green lawn with a few bushes dotted here and there. Maybe she could plant some dog safe flowers, or some herbs in pots along one of the walls. She'd talk to Martha about it later.

After Teddy had romped around, they trooped back into the house. She made herself that promised hot chocolate, and joined Martha on the sofa, Teddy following.

A game show was on the TV.

"It would be fun to be on one of those," Martha commented. Pru noticed she'd finished her mug of hot chocolate.

"It might be," she agreed, although she didn't know if she'd want all those people in the audience to watch her – what if she made a mistake in answering the question?

"You know what I'm gonna do? I'm gonna write to them and see how I can be a contestant!"

Pru stared at her, then giggled. "Why not?"

"Exactly." Martha nodded vigorously.

"But what about your retired lady detective script?"

"You're right – I need to keep working on that," Martha said. "But it's hard to find the time when we've got a murder to solve, plus my usual senior center and café visits, and playing with Teddy." She grinned at him, lying on the carpet next to her feet, his gaze fastened on the television.

"Did you find out anything at the senior center today?"

"Not much." Martha pouted. "Only that no one else had been burgled around the same time as Victor so he could have been making up the whole thing."

Pru told her about checking online for blue shepherdess statues and seeing some like Peggy's, and how much they were listed for.

"That makes it sound even more suspicious that Victor claimed his blue shepherdess was an antique," Martha declared.

They went to bed, Pru's mind buzzing with possible burglary theories.

"Tomorrow when you get home from the library we can visit Mitch," Martha told her, "and see what he thinks about Victor's burglary. We might even bump into Detective Hottie!" She chuckled.

***

After a busy day at the library, Pru was relieved to get home. Then she remembered that Martha wanted to visit the police station.

She hoped they wouldn't run into Jesse. All she wanted to do was sit down on the sofa with a mug of instant hot chocolate, relax, and take a break from thinking about murder and burglaries.

Pru had fielded a lot of reference questions that day. Barbara had to take the art group as their leader hadn't turned up, but all the other members had. And she had not been happy about that. Pru suspected her boss's favorite part of the job was attending to inquiries at the reference desk.

"Ruff?" Teddy appeared wearing his red bandana when she opened the front door.

"Don't you look handsome?" She bent down to stroke him.

"Ruff!" He wagged his tail, happy with the attention.

"I've already told him what a cute boy he is." Martha wheeled her walker along the hall. "And he's coming with us to see Mitch. He won't be able to resist telling us the truth about Victor's burglary when he sees Teddy!"

"You could be right." Pru wondered if that would be the case, but so far she thought Mitch was very professional, and doubted that seeing Teddy wear his bandana would make him spill any secrets.

They piled into Pru's car, and Martha directed her to the police station, although she knew the way by now.

"And then we can get pizza for dinner," Martha declared. "If that's okay with you. I don't feel like cooking tonight and it's my turn, so I thought we could switch the nights over to pizza night."

"That sounds good." Her mouth watered at the thought. It had been hours since lunch, and she hadn't had time for a snack before they'd set off.

After pulling up at the curb, Pru got out Martha's walker from the trunk, and snapped on Teddy's lead.

"How's your hair?" Martha peered at her in a scrutinizing way. "I guess it will do. But you're not wearing your lipstick." She sounded disappointed.

"No, I'm not," she said agreeably.

"Well, I guess you don't really need it." Martha barreled into the station, Pru and Teddy right behind.

"We'd like to talk to Mitch," she informed the young uniformed officer behind the counter.

"Detective Denman is very busy, ma'am," he replied. "I'll have to check—"

"Yoo hoo, Mitch!" Martha waved as Mitch strode down the staircase and halted on the bottom step.

"Martha. And Pru." He looked a little relieved when he spied Pru.

"Ruff!" Teddy wagged his tail.

"And Teddy." He smiled briefly.

"Where's Detective Hot – Jesse?" Martha asked.

"He's gone home."

"Oh." She sounded disappointed.

"What can I help you with?" he asked.

"We wanna know about Victor's burglary," Martha told him. "Was it real or was it faked?"

Mitch blinked at them. "Why are you asking about it?"

"Because we want to find out who killed Victor," Martha replied. "This is a case for the senior sleuthing club!"

"We think that maybe Victor lied about being burgled," Pru put in, "so he could say that his blue shepherdess statue was an antique and claim on the insurance."

"Whether he had a blue shepherdess or not," Martha put in. "He had insurance, right?"

"He mentioned it," Mitch admitted. "I told him to put in a claim for his stolen items."

"What else did he have stolen?" Martha's eyes lit up.

"A few small items – a watch, an expensive pen and – I'd have to check the report for anything else. Plus the blue shepherdess statue."

"Do you think his house really was broken into?" Pru asked.

"If it wasn't, he did a good job of faking it," Mitch admitted. "A back side window was broken, and the glass was on the inside."

"Ooh – maybe he was a burglar in real life!" Martha sounded excited.

"We've never suspected him of wrong doing," Mitch said a trifle sternly. "So please don't share that theory around town, especially when Victor is no longer here to defend himself."

After a moment, Martha nodded. "Yeah, you're right. Sorry."

"Is there anything else I can help you two with?" he asked.

"Was the blue shepherdess really an antique, if it did exist?" Pru asked. "I've had a brief look at online auction sites but the ones I found seem similar to Peggy's, mass produced, and not worth much."

"We haven't heard anything about a valuable blue shepherdess floating around," he replied.

"Who inherits his house?" Martha asked.

"That would be a matter for his lawyer to tell you," Mitch said.

"So he does have a lawyer," Martha pounced.

"Yes," he admitted. "And that's about all I can tell you right now. I'm sure we'll find Victor's killer soon. I don't want you putting yourselves into any danger." He looked down at the dog. "That goes for you, too, Teddy."

Teddy made a little wuffing noise, his tail wagging as he looked up at Mitch.

"If you'll excuse me, I'm going home. It's been a long day."

Pru noticed shadows under Mitch's eyes and sympathized.

"Tell Lauren her cupcakes were delicious as usual," Martha said.

"I will." His expression lightened at the mention of his wife. "If I'm lucky, she'll have saved me some for tonight." He nodded goodbye and left the building.

"I guess we'll have to snoop around and find out who the lawyer is," Martha declared.

Pru noticed the desk officer's eyes widening, and tilted her head toward the exit.

"Good idea." Martha nodded. "We don't want anyone overhearing our plans."

She just hoped the officer didn't think they were up to no good.

When they got home, Martha said, "I think we should order that pizza now."

"Ruff!"

It was Pru's turn to choose, and she selected a new combination – pepperoni and pineapple. When the pizza arrived, the tempting aromas filled the small duplex, making Pru's stomach growl.

"This was a good idea," Martha mumbled around a mouthful. "We've got pepperoni which is just the tiniest bit spicy, plus the sweet pineapple. And we got the senior discount."

"It's delicious," Pru said after another bite.

"Ruff?" Teddy also sat at the table looking from Martha to Pru and back again, his brown eyes hopeful.

"Sorry, little guy, but pepperoni's not good for you. It might upset your tummy. And you've already had your dinner – those meaty beef chunks."

Teddy didn't look convinced.

"What if Teddy chooses something to watch on TV later?" If anyone had told her five months ago she would say something like that before she'd met Martha and Teddy, she would have laughed. Now, it seemed pretty normal to suggest such a thing.

"Good idea." Martha's eyes lit up. "I bet he'd like that. I can scroll through the shows and Teddy can bark when he chooses one. What do you say, little guy?"

"Ruff!" *Yes!*

"So the next task for the senior sleuthing club is to find this lawyer who handled Victor's will, so we can find out who inherits," Martha said after finishing her share of the pizza.

"How are we going to do that?"

"I can ask around at the senior center again."

"Don't people there sometimes wonder at all your questions?"

"Sometimes," Martha admitted. "But they also know I like catching up on all the gossip. It's amazing how much goes on in a small town like Gold Leaf Valley. And they know I like sleuthing – well some of them do, so they don't mind if I ask them if they've heard of Victor, and what did they think of him, stuff like that."

"What about Cynthia?" Pru said. "Shouldn't we talk to her again?"

"Yep," Martha replied. "And we've gotta track down this Brian – Victor's friend at the garage sale. Maybe he knows something about Victor no one else does."

"Maybe they grew up together," Pru suggested.

"Good one." Martha pointed to Pru. "Yeah, that might be it."

Teddy ended up choosing a movie about a girl raising horses, which had a happy ending. Pru enjoyed the sweet film, but couldn't stop yawning by the time it finished.

"I know." Martha nodded. "Sleuthing can take it out of you. We'd better get to bed because we've got more snooping around to do tomorrow."

CHAPTER 8

"Well, that was a bust," Martha greeted Pru the next afternoon. "No one at the senior center admitted to knowing who Victor's lawyer is."

"It sounds like he didn't have any close friends here, from the little we know about him," she commented. "I can't imagine him – or anyone – telling people they don't know very well that they've made a will and name the lawyer they used."

"Unless they were afraid they were gonna get killed," Martha mused. "Then they might say that to scare off the killer. Otherwise, I think you're right. Poop."

Pru sat down on the sofa next to her. Teddy sat on Martha's other side, his fluffy white ears tuned into the conversation.

"What's Teddy been up to today?" she asked.

"We had a good play with the ball, didn't we?" Martha stroked the little cotton furball. "And we went to the café." She crinkled her brow. "I might have to stop going there quite so often. I think I've been there every day this week and it adds up fast."

"Why don't I buy the cupcakes next time?" she offered.

"I wasn't hinting, but thanks." Martha smiled. "I've nearly paid off my credit card which is good – your rent money is certainly helping. And now that I have all the different color collars and leads for Teddy, I shouldn't need to spend much on him at the moment, apart from his food of course, and if he needs a new toy."

"What about fabric for his new bandanas?"

"Oh, yeah." Martha nodded. "I forgot about that. Maybe next week I can go to the craft shop and browse. I only need a small amount of material, so it shouldn't be too expensive, even if we get something real fancy for him."

"Ruff!" Teddy looked excited at the thought of a new bandana.

"Now we've gotta talk to Cynthia," Martha directed.

"When?"

"Maybe next week. We've done a ton of sleuthing this week and I might need a little break."

"I understand," Pru replied. It would be nice to take it easy over the weekend, read a book, and take Teddy for walks. She wondered if Jesse had finished reading that thriller he'd borrowed from the library and if it was any good, then instantly told herself not to think about him.

"Maybe I can work on my retired lady detective script." Martha brightened. "Yeah – I can get you to act out some scenarios."

"Me?" Pru blinked. "What sort of scenarios?"

"Nothing dangerous – I think. I've gotta come up with something first. But you might need to practice some yoga poses."

"Why would I need to practice yoga for your script?" She hadn't done much yoga for a while now, something she felt a little guilty about.

"Oh, you know." Martha waved a hand in the air. "You might have to dodge out of the way suddenly. See, I've got those two hot shot detectives who aren't so hot trying to solve the case and they get in my retired lady detective's way. So she's gotta put them in their place."

"By doing yoga?"

"I've got to work it out all up here first." She tapped her head. "Then write it down, and get you to act it out."

"As long as it's not dangerous," Pru felt compelled to say.

"If it is, I'll call Detective Hottie right away for help!"

***

The next afternoon, Pru relaxed on the sofa lengthways, reading a cozy mystery, Teddy in her lap, when Martha suddenly appeared, wheeling her walker.

"I've got it!" Martha announced.

"What?" Pru looked up.

"Ruff?" Teddy asked.

"I've come up with an idea for my script. But I'm not sure if it's gonna work. So I thought we could go to the park and act it out."

"Exactly what are we going to act out?" And by we, Pru had a sinking feeling Martha meant *her*.

"What my retired lady detective does," Martha said airily.

"Does this involve yoga?"

"It might."

"Is Teddy doing something in this scene?"

"Not yet," Martha replied, "but you never know – a great idea might strike me when we're out in the fresh air and feeling my script."

"Ruff!" Teddy jumped off Pru's lap and trotted toward the front door.

"See? Teddy wants to help," Martha said.

"Okay." Pru placed her bookmark in the novel and rose. "Maybe we should drive there."

"Good idea." Martha nodded. "I've walked all over town this past week and I need to pace myself."

They piled into Pru's car and she drove the few blocks to the park. She felt a little guilty driving the short distance, but she had no idea what Martha had in store for her. She hoped it wasn't too strenuous.

After parking in the small lot, Pru got out Martha's walker from the trunk.

"Do you have your script?"

"It's right here." Martha patted the walker basket. "Don't worry. I know what I'm doing."

Pru hoped so.

After clipping on Teddy's leash, they set off to the middle of the park. A few families played with their children on the swing sets a short distance away, but otherwise they had the space to themselves. The day was a little chilly but the sun struggled to peek out behind gray clouds. The green lawn and oak trees made it a pleasant place to spend time.

"Here is a good spot." Martha halted next to a big rock. "Those two hot shots try to pull another trick on my lady detective, but she outsmarts them."

"How?" Pru couldn't help being intrigued.

"That's what you get to act out!" Martha's eyes gleamed. "Go behind that rock and then pop out when I tell you to. See, it's nighttime in my script and those two hot shots think it's fun to scare her away from the scene of the crime. So she hides behind this rock and BOO! She jumps out and scares them. They scream in fright and race off to their car, and she can't stop laughing."

"That does sound interesting." If Martha's script was ever made into a TV show, she'd know she would definitely watch it.

Pru walked behind the rock and bent down to hide herself. The grass was a little scuffed up and she could see some dirt. Something glinted in the soil and she bent down further. What was it?

"Pru," Martha hollered, "jump out from behind the rock and yell 'Boo!'"

Her fingers touched the gritty dirt and she brushed it away from the object that glinted. Her eyes widened and she gingerly touched the short wooden handle.

"Pru!" Martha shouted. "You've gotta jump out now and yell 'Boo!'"

"Ruff!"

She pulled the penknife out of the dirt and came out from behind the rock, not bothering to jump out or say boo.

"Look what I've found." She held out the small penknife to Martha.

"That's not the murder weapon," Martha sounded disappointed. "We saw it lying on the ground next to Victor."

"But it reminded me we haven't asked Mitch if he found any fingerprints on that knife."

***

"I'm gonna call him right now." Martha plunked down on the seat of the walker and speed-dialed Mitch.

"Hi, Lauren," Pru heard her say. "Is Mitch around? Uh-huh. Yeah, I wouldn't normally bother him on the weekend," unfortunately Pru didn't know if that was true or not, "but I've just thought of something I need to ask him. I'll be real quick." A pause. "I promise."

Pru felt a pang of sympathy for Mitch. He was probably trying to relax and enjoy his time at home with Lauren and Annie.

"Mitch, whose fingerprints did you find on the murder weapon?" Martha asked him. "None? Are you sure? Huh. Okay. Thanks. Yes, that's all. What am I up to?" Martha sounded innocent. "We're at the park and Pru is acting out a scene from my retired lady detective script. Yeah. Hold on." She held out the phone to Pru. "He wants to talk to you."

"Me?" She gingerly took the device. "Hi, Mitch. Yes, we're at the park with Teddy. I found a penknife partly buried in the dirt. Okay. Bye."

After ending the call, she handed the phone back to Martha. "He wants us to turn in the penknife on the way home."

"I don't know why," Martha grumbled. "It's not the murder weapon."

"Maybe it was used in some other crime," she suggested. "Or someone's lost it and told the police station about it."

"Or maybe he doesn't want it lying around the park in case children pick it up," Martha added. "Okay. But first you've gotta act out my script for me." She paused. "Please?"

It was the *please* that touched Pru. "Okay."

She walked behind the rock again and when Martha shouted for her to jump out and say boo, she did, with a loud voice and a fierce expression on her face.

"That was good." Martha nodded. "You nearly scared me and I knew it was coming."

"I hope Teddy wasn't afraid." She glanced down at the Coton, who sniffed her sneakers.

"I warned him what was gonna happen so he wouldn't be scared. I told him we were playing a game."

"Ruff!"

"Do you have any more scenes you'd like me to act out?" Pru asked.

"Not yet. But now I know this bit works, I've got to come up with more story."

"I understand. How far along is this script? Halfway?"

"Nearly." Martha looked a little chagrined. "I've been working on it for a while, too. I've really got to get going with it again."

They stopped by the police station on the way home, handing in the pen knife and explaining how they found it. The officer on duty thanked them and bagged it, typing a note into the computer.

It was Pru's turn to cook that night and she decided on roasted chicken portions with sweet potato and onions.

"This is yummy," Martha praised, tucking into her meal. "You can make this again and again."

"Thanks." It was one of her Mom's recipes. Sometimes she missed her family in Colorado, but working at the library here in Gold Leaf Valley was the only job offer she'd received, especially after the cheating scandal that had rocked her world in college.

When she'd finally explained it to Martha a few months ago, she and Teddy had been very understanding, but unfortunately the whole debacle had made her a little wary of friendships and trusting people.

"Do you ever hear from that so-called best friend of yours who used you to cheat and then blamed it all on you?" Martha patted her lips with a cloth napkin.

Pru stared at her. "Are you a mind reader?"

"You looked a little sad just then and I knew it couldn't be eating your dinner that caused that expression."

"The thought of her had just popped into my mind," she admitted. "And no, I haven't heard from her at all."

"Good." Martha nodded. "You don't need someone like that in your life. She hung you out to dry and everyone who's met you must know you wouldn't do something bad like that. Don't worry, there are lots of good people in Gold Leaf Valley."

"As well as murderers."

"That's true. But you've gotta take the good with the bad. And since I've lived here, I've met a lot more good people than bad. You'll see."

"Thanks." Pru smiled at her, surprised to find her eyes a little misty. She had been lucky to become Martha and Teddy's roommate.

They watched another spy drama on TV that evening, Teddy sitting between them on the sofa.

"She's got the right idea." Martha nodded at the actress on the screen, karate chopping her frenemy who'd just betrayed her. "She's not putting up with any nonsense."

Pru thought maybe she could take some life lessons from both Martha and the spy drama. And maybe Teddy as well.

CHAPTER 9

After a relaxing Sunday, where they didn't do any sleuthing or act out any more of Martha's script, Pru drove to the library the next day. She hoped her boss Barbara would be in a good mood.

After firing up the computer, she started scanning the books that had plopped through the book drop on the weekend.

"Pru." Barbara appeared a while later, dressed in a dark suit and crisp white blouse. "I need you to open the boxes of new books that are scheduled to arrive today. I've had patrons clamoring for them all last week." She sounded a little annoyed at that.

"Of course." She nodded.

"Oh – and fix up this man, will you?" She pointed to an older man standing near the non-fiction shelves, dressed in jeans and a brown sweater. "He wants to borrow some books but first he needs to become a member."

Her eyes widened when she realized it was Brian.

"Oh – hi," she sounded a little flustered. What should she ask him about the murder and Victor? She wished Martha was here – she was sure her roommate wouldn't have any problems coming up with questions immediately.

"You look familiar." He frowned at her, his wide forehead furrowed.

"The church garage sale a week ago," she prompted.

"That's it." He nodded.

"I'm sorry about your friend," she blurted.

"Thanks. It was the darnedest thing. I hadn't seen Victor for years until we bumped into each other there, and then he died on the same day. What are the odds?"

She took his name and address, noting that it was right in Gold Leaf Valley, and made a laminated card for him. "There you go. You can borrow up to twenty items for three weeks. If the library is closed when you want to return them, you can put them in the book drop outside."

"Thanks." He smiled. "I've got some DIY to do and some of your books might be helpful."

"I hope so." Surely there was a question she could ask him about his friend's murder? "Have you been living here long?"

"A few weeks," he replied. "It's a nice little place, isn't it? How about you?" He peered at her name badge. "Pru."

"I've been here a few months," she replied.

"Are there any groups happening in the library? Maybe I should join something and get to know people."

"We have French, and Greek conversation, plus an art group. The board over there has the listings for everything." She gestured to the bulletin board near the self-check out machine.

"Thanks. I'll take a gander." He wandered over to the bulletin board, and then back to the non-fiction shelves.

The rest of the day was quiet. The boxes of books arrived, and she was able to process them all, much to Barbara's satisfaction. She kept an eye out for Jesse, wondering if he'd finished reading that thriller, but to her disappointment, he didn't come in – unless he'd stopped by during her lunch break. She didn't notice the book when she scanned more returns that afternoon.

When she arrived home, she felt tired, and hoped Martha didn't have any strenuous sleuthing planned for them.

"You'll never guess!" Martha sounded excited, and patted the empty seat on the sofa next to her. "You just missed Detective Hottie!"

"What?" She blinked.

"Ruff!" Teddy climbed on her lap.

"He left this book for you." Martha pointed to the thriller on the coffee table. "Said he'd finished it but didn't have time to stop by the library to return it, so he asked if you could."

"He what?" Pru's eyes widened.

"I think he was really using it as an excuse to see you." Martha chuckled. "He seemed disappointed when I informed him you were still at the library. I told him he could wait until you came home but he said he had to check out a lead this afternoon and my house was on his way."

"Huh." She wasn't sure what to think.

"Maybe you should read it." Martha picked up the book and turned to the back cover. "It's about a spy and how he gets into trouble and is on the run but he's a good guy, not a bad one. Sounds pretty good. Maybe I should read it after you."

"Of course." She wondered if she should be annoyed or flattered that Jesse had dropped in his library book.

"So, did anything exciting happen today?" Martha said. "No new gossip at the senior center, and watercolor painting is taking a break for a few weeks. The café is closed on Mondays which is good, so I wasn't tempted to go there and spend money."

"Ruff." Teddy sounded a little sad at that.

"Don't worry." Martha stroked him. "We can go tomorrow. I'll just get a hot chocolate."

"I said I'd spring for the cupcakes next time," Pru remembered. "So what if you buy three to bring home and we can share them?"

"Goody." Martha's eyes lit up. "I'll get one of each again. But you were just about to tell me if something exciting happened at the library today."

"As a matter of fact …" Pru told her about Brian coming in. "He said he's only been living here for a few weeks."

"What else?' Martha asked eagerly.

"He's doing DIY and wanted to know if there any groups at the library he could join."

"And?"

"That's it."

"You didn't ask him anything else?"

"I was so surprised to see him, it was hard to think up something. It's not as if I could ask him if he killed Victor, could I?"

"I guess not." Martha sighed. "Well, maybe *I* could. But never mind – you're still a baby sleuth."

"What about Cynthia?" Pru asked, feeling a little guilty at disappointing Martha with her sleuthing prowess – or lack of it. "Was she at the senior center today?"

"Nope. But we should talk to her and find out more about Victor. And if he ever talked about his friend Brian."

"That is a good idea."

"Thanks." Martha sounded pleased. "We can do that tomorrow. You look a little tired. It's my turn to cook tonight and I'm gonna make one of my specialties – corned beef hash."

"I can't wait." She smiled. Martha was a good cook and they both enjoyed the old-fashioned dish.

Before dinner, Pru tried a few yoga poses, reminding herself to check if there was a studio in town. It was too easy to get out of the habit of a home practice, let alone attending real life classes. Perhaps Lauren and Zoe would know if there were any sessions locally.

The rest of the evening passed pleasantly. She tidied up the living room, sorting out the few magazines Martha had left in various places, and then attended to the dishes and cleaned the sink, leaving it sparkling.

"It's good that you're neat and I'm messy," Martha observed. "It balances everything out." She glanced down at Jesse's returned library book, still lying on the coffee table. "Don't forget to start reading it."

"I won't."

***

Pru blinked and slowly opened her eyes. A thud suddenly jerked her awake, and she rolled over, peering over the side of the bed. Jesse's book that she'd started reading last night lay on the carpet.

She'd only meant to read the first few pages, but she quickly became hooked on the story, although she wished there were more females in it. By the time her eyes had drooped shut while she turned the next page, she'd turned off her bedside light and fell asleep instantly.

"Pru?" A knock on her bedroom door.

"Ruff?" Teddy scratched at the door.

"Are you going to the library today? It's already eight," Martha called.

"It is?" Pru stumbled out of bed and flung open the door, narrowly missing Martha's walker. "Why didn't my alarm go off?" She glanced at the travel alarm clock she'd brought with her from Colorado.

"Maybe you didn't set it properly?" Martha was already dressed in turquoise sweats.

"Ruff?" Teddy trotted into her room and nosed the book on the floor.

"I ended up reading late," she admitted.

"You'd better get dressed and have a bite to eat before you go to work,"

Martha said. "What time do you have to be there? Nine?"

"Yes." She picked up the book and placed it on the bed. "Thanks, Martha."

"No problem," Martha replied cheerfully. "Come on, Teddy, let Pru hop in the shower and get dressed. She's hooked on Jesse's book."

After checking her alarm clock – somehow she had neglected to flip on the alarm – grrr – Pru did as Martha suggested and had a quick shower, and then dressed in gray slacks and a pale blue sweater.

She gulped down her fiber-rich cereal, and waved goodbye to Martha and Teddy.

"We can do more sleuthing when you get home this afternoon," Martha called after her.

***

After a busy day at the library, Pru was eager to get home and relax for a bit. Maybe she and Teddy could play in the garden, or go for a walk around the block. But Martha had other ideas.

"It's sleuthing time," Martha announced as soon as she stepped into the living room. Teddy wore a turquoise collar and lead.

"Ruff!" His brown eyes sparkled and he wagged his tail.

"What are we doing?" She eyed the sofa longingly. Sitting down and watching a game show on TV sounded good right now.

"We're going to the homemade shop to buy Teddy some fabric first," Martha told her. "And then we can decide whether to go to Cynthia's house or Brian's. You should know his address since you made him a library card."

"You're right – I do." She'd forgotten about that detail today because of her late night and day of busy tasks under Barabara's direction. "But is it really ethical of me to show you where he lives because I know that as part of my job, and we're sleuthing in our private time?"

"I thought you might say something like that. Because you've got lots of principles. Which is mostly a good thing," Martha said in approval. "So I thought we could just take Teddy for a walk, and wouldn't you know it, we're strolling past Brian's house!"

"Well, I guess," she said doubtfully. She couldn't really argue with Martha's plan – could she?

"He might even be doing DIY out the front. It would be rude not to say hello to him," Martha continued.

"You do have a point," she conceded.

"Anyway, first I'll buy Teddy some bandana fabric," Martha promised. "Ooh – I bought three cupcakes for us this morning and we can have them for dinner tonight. Although, it was hard not to sample any of them." She sounded proud of her restraint.

"What sort are they?"

"Super vanilla, Norwegian apple, and salted caramel."

"They sound delicious." Her mouth watered at the thought.

"Come on," Martha urged. "The sooner we finish sleuthing, the sooner we can enjoy those cupcakes!"

CHAPTER 10

"What about this color?" Martha fingered a sapphire fabric. "Or this red tartan?"

Pru stood next to Martha and Teddy in the handmade shop. The clerk had allowed the Coton to enter after Martha had explained she wanted Teddy to choose the fabric for his new bandana. The clerk had smiled and said she thought it was a wonderful idea.

"Teddy already has a red bandana," Pru reminded her.

"Oh pooh, you're right." Martha pouted. "And I forgot to put it on him when we were getting ready to leave."

Teddy sniffed the wooden floorboards, and the bottom rack of fabric rolls.

"What about this one?" Pru pointed to an emerald fabric with fawn teddy bears on it.

"Ooh – I like that. Teddy, what do you think?" Martha gestured to the fabric. "Teddy and teddy bears – perfect!"

"Ruff!" Teddy's eyes lit up and his tail wagged.

"I think that means he wants it," Pru joked.

"I think so, too," Martha said seriously.

Pru brought the roll over to the counter.

"How much do I need to make Teddy here a bandana?" Martha asked.

The clerk peered over the counter at the small fluffy dog. "Maybe a fifteen-inch square?"

After cutting the required length, the clerk popped the material into a paper bag for them.

"Thanks." Martha paid in cash, and then looked around the small shop. "You've got yarn, and cross-stitch stuff and—" she gasped "—a blue shepherdess!"

"Where?" Pru swung around from perusing patterned buttons. Her eyes widened as her gaze followed Martha's pointing finger.

A blue shepherdess statue stood serenely on a shelf next to rolls of ribbon.

"Do you like it?" The clerk smiled.

"Where did you get it from?" Pru asked, unable to take her gaze off it.

"It's not Peggy's, is it?" Martha asked.

"Peggy?" The clerk frowned. "I don't know anyone called that."

"Not Peggy's, then," Martha confirmed to Pru. "Which is good because she told us that she was gonna keep hers."

"How long have you had the statue?" Pru asked.

"I found it at a garage sale a few weeks ago at Zeke's Ridge." The clerk mentioned a town twenty minutes away from Gold Leaf Valley, and even smaller.

"Hmm," Martha murmured.

"Peggy did say her blue shepherdess was mass produced," Pru reminded her. "Maybe it was very popular in this area a long time ago and everyone bought one."

"Yeah – maybe they couldn't buy a lot of different figurines around here, in the olden days," Martha agreed. She turned to the clerk, noting the puzzled expression on her face. "Sorry. But your blue shepherdess looks just like my friend's, and her neighbor said he had one that was stolen from his house last month."

"Stolen!" The clerk blanched. "I can assure you that I bought this statue fair and square at that Zeke's Ridge garage sale."

"How much did you pay?" Martha inquired.

"Martha," Pru cautioned.

"Ten dollars," the clerk admitted. "I thought it was a little high to be honest, but I couldn't help myself. I think she suits the shop – don't you think?"

Pru admired the graceful lines of the shepherdess, with her blue frock and little white lamb. "She's very pretty."

"She is," Martha conceded.

The shop door tinkled and they both turned to look at the newcomer. Cynthia stood in the doorway, looking stylish in tweed slacks and a burgundy sweater. The outfit set off the tones of her warm caramel hair nicely.

"Oh, goody." Martha beamed. "We were going to visit you next."

Pru wondered what had happened to the plan to stroll by Brian's house.

"What about?" Cynthia looked interested. "Oh, there's Teddy. What a darling little boy you are."

"Ruff!" Teddy looked pleased at the praise, wagging his tail.

"We were going to ask you about Victor," Martha said.

A hunted look crossed Cynthia's face. "Maybe we should do that outside."

Martha nodded, and said goodbye to the clerk. "We'll wait outside while you do your business," she told Cynthia.

Cynthia stepped up to the counter and said something to the clerk who disappeared out the back. Pru wondered what it was about as she followed Martha outside.

The street was quiet, and when she looked at her watch, Pru was surprised to see it was almost five.

"Stores start closing around now for the most part," Martha commented. "Did you see the look on Cynthia's face?"

"I did."

"I wonder why she looked scared. Do you think she knows more about Victor's death than we thought?"

Before Pru could answer that, Cynthia stepped out of the shop, clutching a brown paper bag.

"My special yarn order," Cynthia explained. "Now ladies, what can I do for you?"

"We wanted to ask you about Victor," Martha told her again. "See, we're investigating his death and we thought we'd ask you some more questions."

"You're not the only ones." Cynthia groaned. "I've had the police ask me countless questions about him. First that good-looking new detective,

Jesse someone. I must admit, I didn't pay attention to his surname, I just enjoyed looking at him." She blushed. "Even at my age, and as a widow, I can still appreciate a good-looking man – even a younger one." She looked knowingly at Pru. "Wait until you're my age, dear. You'll see."

"I know what you mean. That's why I call him Detective Hottie." Martha chuckled. "What type of questions did he ask you?"

"How long I'd been seeing Victor, what did we do on our dates, if I knew Victor before I started dating him. Jesse thought since we both lived in Gold Leaf Valley for years, I might know him socially while my dear husband was still alive. But I told him, no, I was very happy with my husband and I hadn't come across Victor in our close circle of friends here, until he asked me out. Of course I knew who Victor was, it wasn't as if I agreed to go out with a complete stranger."

"Were you ever at Victor's house?" Martha asked eagerly. "Did you see a blue shepherdess statue there?"

Pru thought they were great questions.

"No, I wasn't at his house," Cynthia replied. "And you're not the first person to ask me that. So did Jesse, and then his boss, Mitch."

"Mitch asked you questions, too?" Pru couldn't help herself.

"A couple of days after Jesse did," Cynthia told her. "I got the feeling they weren't getting anywhere, so that's why Mitch decided to interview me himself. But really, I couldn't tell him anymore than I could tell Jesse. Although," she added reflectively, "Mitch is very easy on the eye, too. Lauren is a lucky woman."

"She is." Martha chuckled.

"So is Mitch – a lucky man," Pru was compelled to point out the other side of the equation.

"I think those two were meant for each other," Cynthia agreed, "and the same with Zoe and her husband, Chris."

"Now we just have to find Pru a husband," Martha joked. "I've already got my eye on Detective Hottie for her."

"Martha!" Pru's face flamed.

"Ruff!" Teddy seemed to chide Martha as well.

"Sorry," Martha apologized. "Forget I said that, Cynthia." She patted Pru's arm.

"I won't tell a soul," Cynthia promised. "Is there anything else you wanted to ask me? Like I told you at the church garage sale, after the forgotten wallet stunt Victor pulled on me, I decided not to see him again."

"Did he ever end up paying you back for your date at Gary's?" Pru asked.

"No, he did not." Cynthia shook her head. "And then he had the nerve to ask me out again at the garage sale. I'm afraid we might have attracted a little audience. I don't like to hurt people's feelings, but really, what did he expect me to say? Yes, I'd love to see you again even though I ended up paying for both of us because you were too cheap? That is not how I expect to be treated."

"You've got the right idea," Martha approved.

"Yes," Pru murmured.

Cynthia glanced at her watch. "Is that the time? I must be going. I'll see you at the senior center, Martha."

"You betcha," Martha replied cheerfully.

They watched Cynthia walk away, carrying her bag of yarn.

"Huh," Martha said. "It's a shame she never visited Victor's house and saw a blue shepherdess statue there, so we'd know for sure if Victor had lied about owning one."

"True."

"But now I've got a new idea." Martha grinned. "You can tell Detective Hottie about the blue shepherdess in the handmade shop!"

CHAPTER 11

"It's an excuse to talk to him," Martha continued.

"I don't need an excuse," Pru protested. "I can talk to him on my own – or not talk to him at all."

"What with him missing you when he dropped off his library book at my house, and you not wanting to give him some valuable information, I don't know if you two will ever get together." Martha tsked.

"Who says we want to?" Pru frowned.

"You can't fool me," Martha said. "Just because I've been single for a while – okay, a good long while – and I don't mind it that way, doesn't mean I can't sniff out the beginnings of a romance."

"Why don't *you* tell him about a blue shepherdess statue at this shop?" Pru gestured to the store door behind them.

"Maybe I will." Martha gave a definite nod. "I'll mention it was your idea but you were stuck at the library and couldn't visit him at the police station. Teddy and I will go tomorrow, won't we, little guy?" She glanced down at her fluffy fur baby.

"Ruff!" *Yes!*

"And then after, we could visit Annie at the café. I'll be good and only have a hot chocolate again," Martha said.

"I could buy us some more cupcakes," she offered, wondering if cupcakes nearly every day would be good for her – or not. Even if she practiced yoga regularly again.

"That is tempting," Martha admitted, "but I don't like you paying for cupcakes all the time. Plus, we've got those three we're eating for dessert tonight. Maybe we should limit ourselves to two lots per week – maybe three if we have a crazy sleuthing situation."

"What sort of crazy sleuthing situation?" Pru asked cautiously.

"You never know." Martha waved a hand in the air. "It could be anything at any time, and any location. And we might need lots of cupcakes after that happens."

***

The next day, Pru wondered if Martha would visit Jesse at the police station, just like she said she would. Last night she'd read more of his library book, reluctantly turning off the light when the clock hit eleven p.m.

It was a shame the novel was too big to fit in her purse, otherwise she could have brought it with her and read it on her lunchbreak.

Barbara was busy at the reference desk, leaving Pru free to let her mind drift while she shelved books.

"Pru," a voice whispered near her left ear.

She startled and turned.

"Oh – Doris." She placed a hand over her heart. "It's you."

"Sorry." Doris looked contrite. She wore jeans and a purple sweater, her face flushed. "I didn't want to talk too loudly because of your boss. I know she doesn't like people speaking above a whisper in here."

"You're right about that." She nodded.

"You and Martha are looking into Victor's death, aren't you? That's the gossip around town."

"Yes," she admitted.

"I might have some information for you."

"Really?" Pru stared at her.

"I overheard it at Gary's Burger Diner. That man who's new in town, Brian someone, who was Victor's friend. He was dining there last night and I overheard him tell Cindy, the waitress, that he was going to spend up on his dinner because he'd just come into some money."

"Are you sure?" Pru's eyes widened.

"I had to tell Cindy that someone's order was ready – they'd decided they wanted a plain burger after all when they originally ordered the smoky barbecue special, so we had to remake it. That's why I was just outside the kitchen door, and Brian's table was nearby. And …" she paused.

"And?" Pru leaned forward.

"He wasn't talking in a quiet voice. It was as if he didn't care who heard about his good luck."

"Thanks." Pru smiled. "Martha is going to be delighted to hear this."

"I think it's great that you and Martha are trying to solve the murder," Doris said earnestly.

"You don't think we should leave it to the police?" She still had her doubts at times about interfering with the investigation, but as Martha had pointed out to her, what was the harm of asking her friends and acquaintances some questions?

"They haven't found Victor's killer yet, have they? So why not try finding out who it is yourself?"

"You sound like Martha."

"I hope I'm as spry as she is when I'm her age," Doris replied. "She still gets around, even with her walker."

After choosing a mystery by Krista Davis, Doris scanned it at the self-check out machine, and waved goodbye.

While she continued to shelve books, Pru mulled over the conversation. Was Brian referring to being a beneficiary of Victor's will? That scenario made the most sense. She couldn't wait to tell Martha when she arrived home.

The library was quiet that afternoon, and Barbara let her leave a few minutes early. "You're a good worker, Pru," she said in a rare moment of appreciation. "Enjoy your evening."

"Thanks, Barbara." She smiled at her boss, then drove home in her small, silver SUV.

A black sedan sat parked outside the duplex. Pru frowned as she opened the front door.

"Ruff!" Teddy rushed up to her, his brown eyes gleaming with fun.

"Hello." She bent to stroke him. "What did you do today?"

"Pru? We've got company," Martha called from the living room.

She made her way to the living room, Teddy by her side. Her eyes widened when she glimpsed Jesse sitting on the sofa next to Martha, looking quite comfortable in dark slacks and cream shirt.

"What are you doing here?" she blurted.

"Martha tempted me with a cup of hot chocolate," he admitted.

"It *is* cold outside," she replied.

"I was walking home and spotted Jesse driving past. That made me realize I'd forgotten to pop into the police station to tell him about the blue shepherdess at the handmade shop, so I waved him down, and he drove me the rest of the way home," Martha explained in satisfaction.

"I figured it would be just as easy to take Martha's statement here, than invite her back to the station," Jesse said.

"That was nice of you."

"Get yourself a cup, Pru, and we can both tell Jesse about it," Martha said. "We just did some chit-chatting while we sipped."

"Your hot chocolate is pretty good, Martha," Jesse commented.

"It's from a mix." Martha chuckled. "Not as good as Lauren's at the café, but not bad when you're home."

Pru headed to the kitchen, Teddy at her feet. "Do you want something?" Glancing at his bowl, she noticed it was empty, so she put some beefy chunks in, and topped up his water.

After quickly making hot chocolate for herself, she rejoined Martha and Jesse in the lounge, telling herself they were not butterflies in her stomach, merely hot chocolate yearnings.

"And then we saw a blue shepherdess on a shelf in the handmade shop, didn't we, Pru?" Martha said.

"We did." She sat on the opposite sofa. Teddy trotted into the living room, and sniffed everyone's shoes.

"The clerk said she bought it at a garage sale – in Zeke's Ridge," Martha continued. "So you should pay her a visit and see if she can tell you anything else. It cost her ten dollars."

Jesse wrote something down on a small notepad. "Thanks, Martha." He glanced at Pru.

"Doris told me something today at the library." She cupped her hands around the warm mug and proceeded to tell him the story of Brian saying he had come into some money.

"Ooh – do you think he inherited Victor's loot?" Martha leaned forward eagerly.

"Loot?" Jesse sounded like he was trying not to chuckle.

"You know, everything Victor owned, like the house," Martha continued. "Who knows how much he had stashed away. It sounds like he was a real penny pincher, so he could have thousands – even millions! – in his bank account."

"We've looked into his finances," Jesse said, attempting to contain a smile. "And he didn't have millions, but he wasn't badly off."

"I knew it!" Martha crowed. "Didn't I say, Pru, that I bet he's got more money than he makes out – made out."

"You did," she conceded.

"So, did Brian inherit Victor's estate?" Martha pressed.

Jesse drew in a little breath, as if deciding whether to tell them something or not. "No."

"Well, poop!" Martha frowned. "Who did he leave it all to?"

"It's not for me to say," Jesse said after a moment. "Sorry, ladies."

"So where is Brian getting this sudden influx of money?" Martha asked.

"That's something we can ask him," Jesse said. "I need to do a follow up with him, anyway." He glanced at Pru again. "Martha told me you started reading my library book."

"Martha!" Pru glanced at her.

"I was just making conversation," Martha replied innocently.

"Are you enjoying it?" Jesse asked.

"So far," she admitted. "I'll return it to the library when I've finished – I'll make sure it's not overdue."

"Thanks." He nodded.

Martha looked like she wanted to say something, but refrained.

After thanking them again for their information, Jesse got up to leave. Martha and Teddy escorted him to the front door.

"Come by any time, Jesse," Martha said in a loud, cheery voice that drifted down the hall into the living room. "It was fun."

"Ruff!"

CHAPTER 12

"You two are never gonna go on a date if you keep acting like that," Martha chided when she returned from saying goodbye to Jesse.

"Ruff!" Teddy agreed.

"Who said we want to go on a date – I mean, who said *I* want to go on a date with him?"

"Ha! It's a shame you weren't wearing your lipstick," Martha said. "Never mind. I guess you don't really need it. I don't think Jesse noticed whether you were wearing it or not, despite all the times he looked at you."

"He did?"

"That's because you were too busy looking down at your hot chocolate." Martha shook her head. "Not everyone is like your ex-best friend who involved you in her cheating scandal."

"But Jesse doesn't know about it," she said quietly. "What if I tell him one day and—"

"And what? You were totally innocent. If he likes you, he'll understand all about it. Plus, don't forget he's a detective. He's probably seen tons of people get mixed up in crimes that weren't their fault at all." When she noticed the look on Pru's face, she added, "Not that you were mixed up in a crime. Nope."

"Ruff!" Teddy nudged Pru's leg, and she picked him up and placed him on her lap.

"See? Teddy knows a good person when he meets them." Martha beamed at the Coton. "I bet Jesse does, too."

"Maybe," Pru said softly, hoping it was true.

The rest of the evening passed enjoyably. They ordered pizza, watched a costume drama set in the eighteen-hundreds, and then went to bed. Pru picked up Jesse's book, and read a few pages, but soon her eyes drooped shut and she groped for the switch on her bedside light.

Her last thought before drifting off to sleep was that despite all the information they'd gathered, they didn't seem any closer to finding out who killed Victor.

***

The next day, Pru helped a patron check out a tall stack of books on crochet, when she heard a "Psst!"

Looking up, she noticed Martha standing at the entrance.

Her gaze flew to the basket under Martha's walker seat. She remembered the time Martha had wheeled in Teddy for book club, and wondered if it was happening again.

"Don't worry," Martha staged-whispered. "I haven't brought you know who."

The thirty-something patron turned her head to look at Martha, smiled, then gathered up the piles of books and struggled out the door, Martha moving aside to let her pass safely.

"Why are you whispering?" Pru hurried around the desk. "Are you okay?"

"I'm fine," Martha replied. "I was just checking the coast was clear."

"For what?" She crinkled her brow.

"For your boss – Babs."

"You mean Barbara."

"Yeah." Martha nodded. "She can be a bit scary."

"She's okay." Pru felt she ought to defend her boss. After all, she was the only person, along with the library board, who had given her a job after graduating college.

"I thought I'd get some cookbooks."

"They're down this end." Pru led the way to the non-fiction shelves.

When they reached the cooking section, Pru paused. "What type of recipes were you looking for? Chinese, Indian, Thai, British, baking, desserts, soups—"

"I thought I'd just have a look and see if any tempt me," Martha replied. "But nothing too spicy – I sold some of my cookbooks at the garage sale, remember?"

"You did."

"But now I feel like I need some new ones." Martha chuckled. "And if they're library books, I have to return them, so it's a win-win for both of us!"

Pru couldn't help a little laugh.

"What about—" Her eyes widened as she spied a man entering the library.

"What?" Martha craned her neck and followed her gaze. "It's him! Brian! Quick! Hide!"

"Why are we hiding?" Pru muttered, ducking down at the same time as Martha, behind a row of baking books. She hoped Barbara wasn't around – she hadn't noticed her in the library for a while.

"So we can come up with a plan," Martha mumbled from the side of her mouth.

"What sort of plan?"

"What to ask him, since he didn't inherit Victor's loot. So where is this sudden influx of money coming from?"

"Do you really think we should inquire?" Pru said reluctantly. "Now that Jesse told us Brian hasn't inherited, is it really any of our business where he gets his money from?"

"What if he's the burglar?"

"You mean he might have burgled his friend?" Pru stared at her. "Was he even in town when Victor was robbed?"

"Maybe he sneaked in, burgled him, sneaked home, then made a big thing of moving here," Martha replied. "Because he knew the blue shepherdess was a valuable antique, just like Victor said all along."

"But you thought Victor could have made the whole thing up about owning a blue shepherdess statue," Pru reminded her.

"Well, he could have," Martha said defensively. "But he also could have owned it, and it could have been a valuable antique. And since Mitch confirmed it looked like Victor really was burgled, what if this Brian fellow did it?"

"I think I need to sit down," Pru murmured.

"You can sit on here." Martha patted the walker seat. "As long as he doesn't see you." She paused. "What's he doing?"

Pru bobbed up behind the bookcase, then bobbed back down. "He's in the DIY section, browsing."

"That's good." Martha nodded. "Okay. We'll just walk normally along to the DIY, and then pretend to notice him, and then you'll start chatting to him."

"What about?"

"If he was happy with the books he borrowed," Martha replied. "I bet you could talk for hours about books, and then you can show him all the different sections like plumbing, roofing, that sort of stuff. And meanwhile, I'll think up some good questions to ask him."

"Well, I guess." Pru glanced around the large room, but Barbara wasn't there. Maybe she was chasing up book orders in her tiny office off the small foyer.

"Come on." Martha heaved herself up, grabbed the handles of her rolling walker, and trundled over to the DIY section. Pru had no option but to follow, glad there weren't any other patrons around. How would she explain this to them?

They'd just reached Brian when he looked up and noticed them.

"Hi." He smiled, looking respectable in pressed jeans and a black sweater.

"Hi," Pru returned. "Can I help you find anything in particular?" She gestured to the book in his hand.

"I was looking for something on guttering, and this book seems like it might have what I need." He held up the tome on roofing.

Martha nudged her in the ribs.

"How were the other books you borrowed?" she asked.

"I found some of the information I wanted. I bought an older house and it needs some fixing up. Thought I'd do the work myself."

"You sound like your friend Victor," Martha spoke suddenly. "He was always saying he was going to work on his house but didn't seem to get around to it much."

"You knew him?" His gaze grew more interested.

"We weren't pals," Martha admitted. "But I know his neighbor Peggy."

"Ah." He nodded.

"It's good we can borrow books from the library instead of buying them," Martha continued. "The price of everything is going up so much!"

"You're right," Brian replied. "I was just saying to the waitress at the burger place that I've come into a bit of money. It was great knowing I could afford anything I ordered there."

"Oh?" Martha leaned forward.

"I had a little win on the lottery," he confessed. "A few hundred. Enough to treat myself without feeling guilty. Everyone does it. It's not really gambling, is it?"

"Is that all you won?" Martha seemed to realize what she said and added, "I mean, that's great, isn't it, Pru? Sometimes I buy a ticket myself, but I haven't gotten lucky – yet."

"It is," she confirmed, hoping her cheeks weren't flushed. She felt a little awkward and wondered if they should really be asking Brian these questions in the library. What if Barbara appeared and asked her what she was doing?

"I'm afraid it's not enough to hire someone to do the work on my place, though," Brian joked.

"It's a shame you didn't inherit your friend's house," Martha blurted.

Pru felt like clapping a hand over her own mouth.

"I mean," Martha tried to recover, "that's what I heard—"

"Who from?" Brian furrowed his brow. "His neighbor?"

"No, no," Martha said hastily. "It was—"

"Pru," Barbara suddenly appeared, not looking happy at all. "I trust you are helping this gentleman with his book selection?"

"She definitely is," Brian said, holding out the roofing book.

"And she's helping me too." Martha grabbed a book off the shelf. "She's helping me to—" she glanced at the cover "—fix leaky pipes. Yep, I've got a lot of leaky pipes at home."

"Aren't you two roommates?" Barbara's frown deepened.

"That's why she's helping me," Martha explained hastily. "Pru said borrowing a book on work time was a no-no, and she'd have to wait until her lunchbreak and I said that was too long to wait, so I walked all the way over here—" Martha patted the handle of her walker "—so I could borrow the book instead and not take her away from her work."

"Hmm." Barbara looked like she was trying to poke holes in Martha's logic before giving up. "Don't take too long, Pru. There are more boxes of books to unpack before your shift is over."

"Yes, Barbara," she murmured.

"Phew," Martha muttered when Barbara walked over to the reference desk and sat down.

"I'm glad I'm retired," Brian said.

"I'd better borrow this book." Martha placed it on her walker seat.

"Your boss is looking over here. And I'll go and browse the cookbooks as well."

"Good idea." Pru watched her trundle off to the recipe section. Turning to Brian, she asked, "Is there anything else I can help you with?"

"I'm good. Thanks."

With a smile, she returned to the desk and opened a box of books and processed them.

When she peeked out of the corner of her eye, she noticed Barabra was engrossed on the computer, no doubt looking up an obscure reference.

"Here." Martha plunked down three books. "I couldn't resist a British baking book, although I don't know how different their recipes would be to my old ones, and a ribs book. Don't you think it would great if we made ribs one night?" Her face lit up.

"It would." Her mouth started to water. It was almost lunchtime.

"And here's the leaky pipe book," Martha dropped her voice, "in case your boss checks up on you – and me."

"Good thinking."

She scanned the books and handed them back to Martha.

"See you tonight!" Martha waved cheerily and barreled out of the library.

A few minutes later, Brian placed the roofing book on the desk. "I couldn't find anything else that looked useful," he said.

"I'm sorry. Have you checked the computer? Maybe someone has borrowed the book you need. I can reserve it for you."

"Thanks, but this will do for now." He handed over his library card.

After scanning the card and the title, she tucked the due date slip inside the book. "I hope this helps with your guttering problem."

"Me too." He nodded and left.

The rest of the day passed uneventfully. She finished unpacking the boxes of books, and by the time her shift ended, Barbara seemed to be in a better mood. But Pru had no idea how their investigation into Victor's death would proceed now.

CHAPTER 13

"The senior sleuthing club needs to break this case wide open," Martha announced at dinner that night. It was her turn to cook and they'd enjoyed some reheated home-made chicken soup, followed by Eve's Pudding, a recipe from the library book. It contained baked apple pieces with a delicious sponge topping.

"This is amazing," Pru complimented after eating half her bowlful of dessert.

"Ruff?" Teddy sat between them at the table, his eyes big with curiosity as he looked at each of their bowls.

"You've had your dinner, little guy," Martha said.

"Ruff," Teddy said in a disappointed tone.

"Sorry." Martha patted him. "But this British baking book is great," she told Pru. "Lots of recipes I can try, although I've heard of some of them over the years, like scones, of course, and shortbread."

"What about the ribs book?"

"Haven't looked at it yet. But I will!"

"Maybe I'll look at that one, too," Pru said.

"Be my guest. Both books are on the coffee table." Martha jerked an apple sponge laden spoon in the direction of the living room. "But like I was saying, we need to get going with this case."

"I thought we were."

"Yeah, but we're not getting very far." Martha pouted. "We still haven't found out who inherited Victor's house and his other loot. What if that person killed him for their inheritance?"

"I guess the next step would be to find out who Victor's lawyer was," Pru replied.

"Exactly." Martha nodded. "And I know just the person to ask."

***

"I thought we could visit Peggy before you have to go to work this morning," Martha said the next morning over breakfast.

Pru crunched her fiber-filled cereal, which unfortunately was not filled with much flavor. But it was good for her.

"Will we have time?" She put her spoon in the milky bowl.

"If we hustle," Martha said. "Teddy could come. He loves going on outings."

Teddy trotted into the kitchen, a ball in his mouth.

"Wanna come sleuthing?" Martha invited.

Teddy dropped the ball at Martha's feet. "Ruff!" *Yes!*

"We'll have to be quick," Pru warned. "I don't want to be late."

"We'll have plenty of time," Martha assured her breezily.

"Well, okay." Pru rose and rinsed her bowl at the sink, doing the same for Martha's plate which held crumbs of raisin toast, the mouth-watering scent from the toaster drifting through the kitchen.

After getting ready, she waited at the front door for Martha and Teddy.

"What are we going to ask Peggy? If she knows who inherited Victor's estate?"

"Yep," Martha replied cheerfully. "She must know something, dontcha think?"

"But we've already questioned her."

"We haven't asked her flat out if she knew who Victor's lawyer was, did we? Plus, she mightn't have known then who inherited all his stuff, but she might have heard something since. And then she can tell us!"

Pru drove the three of them in her SUV to Peggy's house, sneaking a peek at her watch. They really were pushing it to ask Peggy some questions, drop Martha and Teddy home, and for her to arrive at the library right on time. So far, she'd had a perfect attendance record, and didn't want Barbara to scold her for being a few minutes late. She knew her boss thought punctuality was a virtue.

"Ooh, look!" Martha's shriek of excitement caused Pru to hit the brakes just before they reached Peggy's house.

"What?"

"Ruff?" Teddy asked from the back seat.

"It's the clerk from the handmade shop. Don't know her name, but she's the one with the blue shepherdess from Zeke's Ridge."

"You're right." Pru parked neatly at the curb and turned off the engine.

"I'm gonna ask her if the police talked to her about the statue." Martha clambered out of the car without waiting to get her walker, and hailed the clerk. "Yoo hoo!"

"We'd better go after her." Pru turned around to face Teddy. "We have to get Martha's walker from the trunk."

"Ruff," Teddy said agreeably.

Pru fetched the walker and placed it on the sidewalk, then attached Teddy's leash to his collar and helped him out of the car.

"You're a good boy." She smiled at him, admiring his fluffy white fur that felt, she knew, like soft cotton.

"Ruff!" *Thank you!*

They both turned to glance over at Martha, talking animatedly to the woman who ran the homemade shop.

"Pru, come over here," Martha directed.

Pru left the walker where it was, and she and Teddy joined them.

"Amanda here was telling me that the police did check her blue shepherdess that she got from that Zeke's Ridge garage sale, but they told her it wasn't valuable."

"So it looks like it's not the one who belonged to that man who died, Victor," Amanda confirmed.

"Unless he was lying about it being valuable in the first place, just like I suggested previously," Martha commented.

"What if the burglars stole it because they thought it might be worth something, and their contact – or fence – said it wasn't worth much, and they sold it at that garage sale in Zeke's Ridge?" Pru suggested.

"The police told me they checked out the family who held that garage sale and they're not known for any criminal activity," Amanda said. "They said that the statue belonged to their grandmother, and she was tired of dusting it, so she told them to sell it for her at their next garage sale."

"Huh," Martha muttered.

"So it's not Victor's blue shepherdess," Pru confirmed.

"Ruff!"

"Well, thanks, Amanda," Martha said. "At least we've cleared up that part of the mystery. Now we have to find out who inherited all of Victor's stuff." She peered at Amanda hopefully. "You don't happen to know, do you?"

"No," Amanda said regretfully. "I wish I did. Victor came into my shop once, and argued about the price of everything, before walking out without buying a single thing. I think he was interested in making his own curtains because he claimed it would be cheaper, and said he'd found an old sewing machine he picked up for practically nothing, but told me on his way out of my shop he'd go to the thrift store where he was sure he could get a much better deal."

"That sounds like him, alright," Martha said.

They said goodbye to Amanda, who said she was on her way to open up the store.

Martha held Teddy's lead while Pru fetched the walker a few steps away.

"Come on," Martha said. "We've gotta ask Peggy some questions!"

"And then I have to go to work," Pru said, but Martha was already barreling up Peggy's path, and didn't seem to hear.

***

"I'm afraid I don't know who Victor's lawyer was," Peggy told them a few minutes later. They stood on her front porch, Teddy wagging his tail.

"Aren't you cute?" Peggy bent down to stroke him. "Yes, you are."

184

"Ruff!" *Thank you!* Teddy wriggled with delight.

"Have you heard who inherited his house?" Martha jerked a thumb at the slightly ramshackle dwelling next door.

"Yes," Peggy held a triumphant note in her voice. "You will not believe it!"

"Who? What?" Martha leaned forward eagerly.

"He left it to the church!"

"You mean Father Mike?"

"Yes, indeed." Peggy nodded. "At least, that's what I heard yesterday from my friend Alicia, who got it first hand from Father Mike himself."

"No!" Martha sounded suitably impressed. She turned to Pru. "You know what this means – we've gotta talk to Father Mike!"

CHAPTER 14

"We are not talking to Father Mike this morning." Pru put her foot down. It was already nudging nine o'clock and she had to be at work in three minutes. There was no way she was going to get there in time.

"Oh, poop," Martha grumbled. "But you're right. You don't want to get on the wrong side of your boss. Thanks, Peggy." She waved goodbye and urged Pru down the garden path and back to the car.

"You can drop me and Teddy off at home," Martha directed. "Sorry that took a bit longer than I thought. But we didn't know we were going to bump into Amanda."

"No, we didn't." Pru looked at her roommate a trifle suspiciously, but she was probably being paranoid.

After dropping Martha back at the duplex, she pressed down on the accelerator and drove the few blocks to the library, making sure she was just under the speed limit.

She rushed into the library four minutes late. Barbara stood at the desk, tapping her foot.

"Really, Pru, is it too much to ask you to get here on time?"

"I'm sorry, Barbara," she replied, feeling that was a little unfair, since it was the first time that she'd been tardy.

"Well, never mind," Barbara brushed off her apology. "You need to set up for French conversation this morning, and then that art group is coming in again." She shook her head. "I'm far too busy to supervise them, so you will have to keep an eye on them and make sure they do not use any paint. Pencils only."

"Okay," she replied.

While she set up the room for the language group, she wondered when she and Martha would visit Father Mike to ask him about inheriting Victor's estate – well, the church inheriting it. She still couldn't believe it – was Peggy's piece of gossip correct?

When it was finally time to clock off for the day, she was relieved. She had the whole weekend to herself – apart from sleuthing with Martha and Teddy, and she wanted to finish reading Jesse's library book before it was due.

When she arrived home, she spotted an unfamiliar older style car outside.

"Ruff!" Teddy greeted her at the front door.

"Come in and have a bite to eat with Father Mike," Martha's voice sounded from the living room.

She blinked, and headed down the hall, Teddy by her side.

"Hi, Pru." Father Mike smiled. Dressed down in jeans and a slightly threadbare olive sweater, he held a plate on his lap dotted with cake crumbs.

"I decided to try making lemon drizzle cake from that recipe book," Martha informed her, "and it's delicious! Even though I do say so myself."

"It definitely is," Father Mike told her. "Please, join us."

"It does look tempting." Pru eyed the rectangular cake crusted with what looked like lemon juice and granulated sugar.

"This British baking book talks about how nice it is to invite friends over for afternoon tea, so I decided to ask Father Mike." Martha cut her a generous slice and handed it to her on a plate.

"And I had some spare time this afternoon, so I gratefully accepted," Father Mike said.

"Father Mike told me about the church inheriting Victor's estate, and I was just congratulating him," Martha continued.

"It was a big surprise," Father Mike admitted. "I can't even remember seeing Victor at a church service. But the funds will be very welcome."

"What are you going to do with Victor's house?" Pru asked.

"I'll sell it," Father Mike said. "The will said that everything is to go to the church here in Gold Leaf Valley. After using a little of the money for necessary church repairs, the rest will be given back to the community in the form of food parcels, and if people need help with their bills, that sort of thing."

"That sounds wonderful." Pru finished a piece of the cake. The tangy lemon contrasted perfectly with the soft sponge and melted in her mouth.

"Detective Hottie wouldn't tell us who inherited," Martha grumbled.

"Detective who?" Father Mike blinked.

"Oops – sorry, Father." Martha looked chagrined. "I mean Jesse, the new detective in town."

"I see." Father Mike smiled slightly. "Well, now you know, Martha, but I suspect you had an inkling before you invited me over today."

"You should be a sleuth, too!" Martha praised. "Do you want to join my senior sleuthing club?"

"That would be tempting," Father Mike replied kindly, "but I'm afraid I have too much to do as it is."

"Wuff," Teddy mumbled, appearing with a slightly battered toy bear, dropping it at Father Mike's feet.

"What's this?" Father Mike asked him gently.

"Ruff." Teddy nudged the brown bear onto Father Mike's shoes.

"Do you want Father Mike to play with you?" Pru asked.

"Ruff." *No.*

Pru had a sudden brainwave. "Father Mike, how's Mrs. Snuggle?"

"Ruff!" *Yes!*

"She's very well, thank you." Father Mike smiled. "We watched Zoe's princess movie again last night, as Mrs. Snuggle loves seeing herself on the screen."

"Teddy, do you want to give your toy to Mrs. Snuggle for a while?"

"Ruff!" *Yes!* Teddy rose on his hind legs and turned around in a circle.

"Well, I'll be." Father Mike admired the little dog's antics. "That is very kind of you, Teddy, and I'm certain

Mrs. Snuggle will appreciate your toy. I'll make sure she returns it to you soon."

"I've only seen him twirl around like that a couple of times," Martha spoke. "What a good boy you are, little guy."

Pru's eyes grew a little misty. "You have a kind heart, Teddy."

"Ruff!" Teddy sat on his haunches, looking pleased.

Father Mike picked up the bear and put it on his lap. "All ready to take home to Mrs. Snuggle," he told the Coton.

"Ruff." Teddy seemed to smile.

***

"I definitely need some cupcakes today," Martha said the next morning. Pru had just finished breakfast, wondering if tomorrow she should give in to temptation and try Martha's raisin toast.

"The café is open this morning, isn't it?"

"Yep," Martha said cheerfully. "I think we should get three treats again – don't you? And share."

"Good idea."

"Ruff?" Teddy looked up from chewing his toy rope.

"I can take Teddy with me," she offered.

"How about we all go?" Martha suggested. "We can update Lauren and Zoe – and Annie, of course – about the case."

"Okay." It would be nice to see them, and she could relax over a latte. "Should we walk there?"

"I guess." Martha sighed. "I know it's good for me, but sometimes its easier to be driven places, since you've got a car." She paused. "Let's do it – let's walk. It will be nice for Teddy as well to stretch his legs."

They set off, Pru holding Teddy's lead while Martha steamrolled along with her walker.

"I'm gonna have a big hot chocolate with plenty of marshmallows. Lauren and Zoe know just how I like it! Maybe a cupcake as well – and we could still buy three to take home. Ooh – maybe we could share a cupcake there this morning – yeah. What do you think?"

Pru paused as they reached the edge of the sidewalk. They had to cross the road and she checked right, left, right again, before answering. "I think that's a great idea." She stepped off the curb with Teddy and Martha.

"Ruff! Ruff!" Teddy turned his head and quivered, his body on full alert.

A black car raced down the road, straight at them!

"Martha!" Pru jumped back, pulling Martha and Teddy with her.

The car fishtailed, the roar of the engine drowning out all other sound as it sped away.

She couldn't speak for a moment, her heart jumping around in her chest.

"Are you okay?" She looked at Martha.

"I gotta sit down." Martha felt for the walker seat and sank down slowly. "Teddy, where are you?"

"Ruff!" *Here!* He nudged Martha's leg.

"He's all right," Pru said. "All of us jerked back in time to avoid being hit."

"He had no right racing down the road like that." Martha sounded more like her old self. "He – or she – could have hit us!"

Pru glanced around but none of the neighbors had popped out of their houses to see what had happened. Perhaps it wasn't the first time they'd heard a noisy car barrel past?

"I'm gonna call Detective Hottie and tell him." Martha felt under the seat and pulled out her phone. "Did you get the license plate?"

"No, unfortunately." She'd been too busy making sure they got out of the way. "Do you have Jesse's number?"

"No." Martha frowned. "But I've got Mitch's." She dialed and told him briefly what had happened. "He wants to talk to you."

Pru took the phone. "Yes, we're okay. I think we can manage. All right, thanks."

195

"Well?" Martha looked at her expectantly.

"He said to take it easy and go home. He'll check the database but since we only have a description of a black car – was it a sedan or something else? – there's not much he can do apart from telling the officers to keep an eye out for a vehicle matching your description."

"Which wasn't much of one, because everything happened so fast," Martha replied. She patted Pru's arm. "Thanks. I don't know what would have happened if you weren't with us."

"But I was." Pru touched Martha's shoulder, and stroked Teddy. "You don't think …" she began slowly, not liking the thought that had just entered her head.

"What? That it was intentional?"

"Yes." Pru stared at her.

"Ruff!"

"Teddy thinks so, too." Martha nodded. "That means we must be on the right track. Maybe we've even spoken to the killer and haven't realized!"

CHAPTER 15

They walked home slowly. Pru offered to run back home and get her SUV, but Martha thought there was safety in numbers.

"You're right," she agreed.

When they arrived at the little duplex, Pru made a hot chocolate for both of them.

"Thanks." Martha wrapped her hands around the mug and smiled shakily. "That near miss took more out of me than I thought."

"Me too." Pru sat down next to her on the sofa. She'd given Teddy a treat in the kitchen while making the drinks. "So who tried to run us over? If it *was* a deliberate attempt?"

"Let's see." Martha took a big sip. "Cynthia, Peggy, Amanda, Brian – who else?"

"Do you really think it was Amanda from the craft shop?" Pru set down her mug on the coffee table. "She told us that she bought her blue shepherdess fair and square from a garage sale at Zeke's Ridge."

"Unless she was lying," Martha said. "But no – why would she? All we'd have to do is check with Mitch – or Jesse – to see if she was telling the truth."

"The same with Peggy telling us that the church inherited Victor's estate, before Father Mike confirmed it," Pru said.

"Unless Peggy has another motive. Maybe she was the person who burgled Victor's house!"

"Why would she do that?"

"Ruff!" *Why?*

"Because she knew Victor really did have a valuable blue shepherdess, and she knew hers wasn't, and she wanted the valuable one as well!"

"Wouldn't the police have questioned Peggy about the burglary?"

"She told them she was out. But what if she was lying, and actually was the burglar?" Martha said triumphantly.

"I thought you liked her."

"I do." Martha sounded conflicted. "And sometimes I like our other suspects as well, in this case and the last one. I like Cynthia. But that doesn't mean they could be totally innocent. Sometimes they trick you."

"I guess so." She thought back to the mysteries she'd read. Martha could be right.

"But how are we going to discover if Peggy stole Victor's valuable blue shepherdess? If he really had one, and it was worth something," Pru asked.

"That's a toughie." Martha took a gulp of hot chocolate. "We might have to do a teeny bit of burglaring ourselves."

"A teeny bit of what?" Her stomach dropped and she wrapped her palms around her mug for instant warmth. "No way!"

"Hear me out," Martha said. "Maybe we don't even have to do the breaking and entering. We could just look through her windows – yeah. And you with your yoga, you could do

that tree pose you were telling me
about a while ago, and give me a
boost. Or you could give yourself a
boost on my walker seat – yeah! And
just peer in through Peggy's windows
and see if you can see anything – like
two blue shepherdess statues! Then
we'd know that she stole Victor's."

Pru glanced down at Teddy, who
looked back doubtfully at her.

"When would we be doing this
peering? During the day?"

"Of course not," Martha replied.
"We'd be spotted."

"But how are we going to see
anything at night? Unless Peggy has
lights on and the curtains pulled
back?"

"Huh." Martha pondered for a few
seconds. "You have a point. Unless
we can shine a torch in through her
window – if she hasn't drawn the
curtains yet."

"Wouldn't it be easier just to visit
her? I know!" Pru's gaze landed on
the British baking book on the coffee
table. "You could make her
something from that library book and

take it over to her. If she invites us inside, we could try to have a look around – somehow."

"You're a genius!" Martha grinned. "That is a great idea! And I can try a new recipe from that book as well!"

"Ruff?" Teddy cocked his head.

"I know what you're thinking, little guy," Martha said. "How are we going to have a good look around inside Peggy's house?"

"Ruff!" *Yes!*

"I've gotta come up with something," Martha said. "Maybe I should think like my retired lady detective would when she has to outsmart those two not so hot shots in my script."

Martha pondered. "I've got it! Teddy can act real cute and distract Peggy, while you go looking through her house for a blue shepherdess. I'll stay with Teddy and talk to her non-stop and between the two of us, she won't even know you're missing!"

"Couldn't we do it the other way around?" Pru asked hopefully. "I'll talk to her and you snoop through her house?" She couldn't believe she was even suggesting such a thing.

"That might be a bit obvious. I know! You can ask to use her bathroom – they do it in the movies all the time – and then you can have a quick snoop. Make sure you check her bedroom – the valuable blue shepherdess might be in there."

"If she did steal Victor's blue shepherdess," Pru reminded her. "And that's if Victor actually had a blue shepherdess statue."

"True." Martha nodded. "I guess we'll find out one way or another this afternoon!"

***

Martha looked through her baking book and decided to make gingerbread.

"We'll take it over to her as soon as it's ready," Martha declared. "It will still be daylight then, so it won't look suspicious. And it will be freshly baked. Peggy won't suspect a thing!"

Pru tried to concentrate on finishing Jesse's library book, but the occasional bang from the kitchen distracted her, as well as her upcoming mission of snooping through Peggy's house to discover if she indeed had two blue shepherdess statues.

Putting the novel down on the sofa, she joined Martha in the kitchen, appreciating the scents of cinnamon and cloves. "Do you need some help?"

"Nope." Martha banged the oven door shut. "I just put it in. Had a few problems with this one." She gestured to the mixing bowl with small globs of brown batter, a floury cup, and measuring spoons scattered over the counter.

"Ruff!" Teddy nosed around on the kitchen floor, ending up sniffing Pru's shoes. When he looked up at her, his furry face looked extra white.

"Do you have a bit of flour on you?" She got out a clean tissue, dampened it, and gently wiped his face. "There."

"Thanks. I must have spilled a little on the floor." Martha set the timer. "As soon as this is cooked, we'll visit Peggy."

The delicious aroma of baking gingerbread soon filled the house.

"Maybe I should have made two – one for us as well." Martha bustled into the kitchen with her walker and opened the oven door. "It does smell good." She got the rectangular tray out of the oven and placed it on a wire rack.

"We'd better get ready." Pru checked her watch. She brushed her hair, collected Teddy's lead, and waited for Martha in the living room.

"All set." Martha looked like she hadn't nearly been run over that morning, looking fresh in a fuchsia jogging suit.

Pru helped her wrap up the still warm gingerbread, and they set off.

"Are you sure you don't want me to drive us?"

"I'm sure," Martha replied. "I'm not going to let a little thing like someone trying to run me down stop me and Teddy from getting some exercise."

"Ruff!" The Coton walked confidently ahead of Pru on the lead.

They strolled down the street, then turned the corner. Martha had placed the gingerbread in her walker basket.

"Not far now," Martha puffed a little. "We just have to—" she halted.

"What?" Pru almost skidded to a stop. So did Teddy.

"It's him! Brian!"

"Where?" Her eyes widened when she spied him snipping away at a green bush in a front yard. She'd been so focused on walking along to Martha's directions that she hadn't noticed the street names. This must be where Brian lived!

"Hello." He straightened and greeted them with a smile.

"Just out for a stroll," Pru called.

"Yeah, we're going to my friend Peggy's house." Martha patted the walker seat. "Got something for her."

"Ruff!" Teddy towed Pru toward the white picket fence.

"That library book I borrowed has been very helpful," he told Pru.

"I'm glad."

"Have you fixed your guttering?" Martha asked, following Teddy to the fence line. Behind it stood a small Victorian house painted a faded green.

"Almost," he replied. "Why don't you come and take a quick look?"

"We really should be on our way," Pru said, glancing at the setting sun. "We want to get home before it's dark."

"This will only take a minute," he said persuasively.

"Ruff!" Teddy pulled Pru toward the driveway.

She had to jog after him so he wouldn't pull on his collar too tightly. "Sorry," she panted, "I don't know why he's like this."

"What is it, little guy?" Martha trundled after them. "What are you—"

"Ruff!" Teddy stared at the garage. The door was raised halfway.

There was a black car parked in there, with a muddy license plate.

"You tried to mow us down!" Martha pointed an accusing finger at Brian.

"Let's get out of here!" Pru glanced around wildly, but the street was quiet – and deserted. People were probably already starting to think about cooking their dinner, or staying inside their warm house.

She shivered, and pulled her jacket around her more tightly.

"What are you talking about?" Brian frowned.

"A car tried to run us over this morning," she informed him.

"It wasn't me."

"I don't believe you." Martha narrowed her eyes. "You're the killer! You killed your friend Victor! I'm gonna call Mitch right now!" She pushed up the walker seat and grabbed her phone.

"No, you're not." Brian wrapped his large hand around Martha's. "You're all coming into the garage with me."

He pulled Martha into the garage, not seeming to care when she banged her leg on the walker wheel. "Ow!"

"Ruff!" Teddy dove for Brian's ankle, pulling Pru with him.

Unfortunately, that meant they were all in the dim garage – with the door closing the rest of the way down.

"Let go of me," Martha demanded.

Brian did so, keeping hold of her phone, and shaking Teddy off his foot.

"I've got my phone." Pru felt in her jacket pocket, pulling it out. The battery flashed a low signal and she bit her lip. She'd meant to charge it that afternoon, but had been distracted with Martha's baking noises and reading Jesse's library book. But there should be enough left to make one call.

"Give it to me," Brian ordered. His nice guy façade had already crumbled and now he looked menacing with his full head of gray hair and scowling wide forehead.

"Ruff!" Teddy dove for Brian's ankle again.

"Arggh!" Brian hopped on one leg, his arms flailing, and knocked Pru's phone out of her hand.

She dropped Teddy's lead and reached down for it, but it had skittered under the car.

"Don't move!" Brian picked up a wrench that hung on the wall and held it menacingly over Martha's head. "Or I'll hit Martha so hard, she'll never recover."

"I knew it!" Martha drew herself up, the wrench not touching her springy gray curls – yet. "You're the killer!"

"But why?" Pru asked, her heart hammering. "I thought you were friends with Victor."

"We were," he replied bitterly, shaking Teddy off his foot. "A long time ago – forty years, to be exact."

"What happened?" Martha probed, bending down to stroke the Coton.

"Back then, Victor liked gambling. It started off with small stuff, but he got hooked, and before long, he was owing bookies all over Portland. He always said he'd win back his losses next time, but he got stuck on a bad losing streak, and his debts piled up. When he got a final warning from his main bookie – who didn't have a reputation for being patient with his customers – and turned up at my door with a black eye and broken jaw – he begged me for help."

"But what could you do?" Martha asked.

"While he was gambling his paychecks away, I was saving as much as I could of mine. I wanted to buy my own house one day and lived pretty bare bones to make it happen. He promised to pay me back, and said if he didn't get the money together for the bookie, he didn't think he'd live another week."

"That's terrible," Pru murmured.

"But how would the bookie get his money back if Victor was dead?" Martha asked.

"There was a rumor that this bookie had already killed someone for not paying up. Victor was totally freaked out after his beating. He said if I didn't lend him the money, he'd give the bookie my name and address and tell him to collect from me. And after seeing Victor's battered face, I didn't want to suffer the same fate. So I lent him the money – nearly all of my house deposit savings – and made him sign an IOU. He promised he'd pay me back ASAP."

"And?" Martha asked.

"He skipped town the next day. I went over to his place to check he was okay, and all his belongings were gone. He'd left a note on the kitchen table for me saying everything was taken care of, but he was too freaked out about the bookie to stick around."

"And he never paid you back?" Pru guessed.

"That's right." Brian waved the wrench in her direction. "I tried to track him down but I was broke after he took most of my savings, and private eyes are expensive. Even when I was able to think about tracking him down years later, thanks to the Internet and social media, I couldn't find him online."

"And then you ran into him here, in Gold Leaf Valley?" Martha sounded skeptical.

"I did." He nodded. "I couldn't believe it! The first time was in the bank and he ignored me. He made me wonder if it really was him. I haven't changed much, and he had a little, but I still recognized him. And then at the church garage sale, I knew for sure it was really him. I later found out he altered his surname, which was why I couldn't find him."

"Maybe he never joined social media sites," Pru mused.

"Probably." Brian nodded. "I never got a chance to ask him that. I was too busy asking him to pay me back."

"And he said no," Martha guessed.

"Yep. And I lost it. All those years of scrimping and saving to save up a house deposit gone, because of his gambling addiction. It took me another five years to save up for another down payment on a tiny house, and even then I had a big mortgage. Only when I retired was I able to sell that house, and buy this place here and finally be mortgage free."

"But if his gambling ruined your life, how come you bought a lottery ticket?" Martha asked. "You told us at the library."

"That was the first time. For once, I thought, why not? I couldn't believe it when I won something. But I won't be making a habit of it, that's for sure."

"You never married?" Pru asked.

"Nope." He shook his head. "Victor taking advantage of me like that destroyed my trust in people. We were best friends – or so I thought."

"But what did he say when you asked him to pay you back at the garage sale?" Martha pressed.

"I caught up with him before he left the grounds and said we had to talk. I didn't want anyone overhearing us, so we went to the back of the church hall. The door was open and we went inside.

"Then I asked him to pay me back. He said it happened a long time ago and he was sorry, but he was broke, had to clip coupons to make ends meet, even when he was bragging at the same time about dating that nice widow. And I realized, that deep down inside, he was still the same Victor he'd always been. Selfish. Always put himself first. I hadn't seen that forty years ago, until he skipped town. So I lost it. I couldn't believe he was doing this to me all over again! I saw a knife on the tiny kitchen sink, grabbed it, and stabbed him. I managed to push him away from me and he ended up on the grass just outside. I wiped my prints off the knife with my sweater, and got out of there.

"And now—" he took a menacing step toward them, "—it's your turn. You two know too much."

"Ruff!" Teddy dove for Brian's ankle again.

"Arrgh! No!" His hands flailed around wildly, the wrench no longer threatening Martha's scalp but falling to the ground with a clang.

Martha rammed her walker into his groin, over and over.

"Help! No!" Brian lost his balance, backing into the garage wall, and landing on the concrete floor with a thump.

"Teddy, fetch," Pru commanded, pointing to underneath the car.

Teddy wriggled under the car and emerged, slightly dirty, holding the phone.

"Good boy," Pru praised, giving him a hug. "Martha, are you okay?"

"I will be once I wheel my walker over him to make sure he can't move!"

"I don't think you should do that," she replied, a wobble in her voice. Brian looked like he wouldn't be able to get up for a while. "Why don't you sit down for a minute while I call Mitch?"

"Well, all right." Martha sat on the black vinyl seat, looking shaken. She glowered at Brian, groaning on the floor. "If you make one wrong move, you know what's gonna happen."

"Errrghgah." Brian's eyes drifted shut and he lay still.

EPILOGUE

They didn't end up visiting Peggy that day. Instead, Mitch gave them a ride home.

"Are you two going to be okay?" He looked at them in concern. All three of them sat on Martha's yellow sofa, while Mitch took the opposite chair.

"We'll be fine," Pru told him.

"Thanks for coming." Martha smiled tiredly at him. "Didn't I tell you the senior sleuthing club would crack the case?"

"I wish you hadn't put yourselves in danger," he replied. "We'd already targeted Brian as a person of interest, and had just discovered he'd been friends with Victor years ago."

"But you hadn't arrested him." Martha pouted.

"We needed to gather evidence first."

"Hmm." Martha didn't sound convinced.

"What about Victor's blue shepherdess statue?" Pru wanted to know. "Did he really have one and was it valuable?"

"The strangest thing happened," Mitch replied. "Father Mike was over at Victor's house today, since it was left to the church, and decided to do some gardening. He found a blue shepherdess statue tangled up in one of the overgrown bushes. We figure the burglars must have either dropped it in their haste to leave – maybe they heard a car nearby – or else had a quick look at it while they were escaping and decided to dump it, as they didn't think it was worth anything. He showed a photo of it to a friend who's knowledgeable about antiques and it seems it's mass produced, just like Peggy's."

"That's a shame," Pru said. "The extra funds from the statue would have helped the church."

"The church is going to do all right out of Victor's estate. Don't worry about that." Mitch smiled.

"So how did Victor go from being a gambling addict to being a penny-pinching miser?" Martha asked.

"An extreme experience like being beaten up and in fear of your life can change people," Mitch replied. "I've seen it before. In this case, it looked like Victor's violent beating from the bookmaker shocked him out of his gambling addiction and forced him to live on the down low, as far away from his old life as he could get. Turning into a penny pincher over the years would be another way of trying to escape his past."

"If he hadn't tried to welch on his debt to Brian again, he'd still be alive," Martha mused. "Well, I guess it takes all sorts to live in this world."

"You've got that right, Marth," Mitch agreed.

"Oh – I totally forgot!" Martha pulled up her walker seat and reached inside.

"Ruff?" Teddy inched forward on the sofa cushion, peering into the basket.

"The gingerbread I made for Peggy!" Martha held the wrapped parcel aloft. "Would you like some, Mitch?"

The heady smell of cinnamon and ginger suddenly filled the living room.

"Why not?" Mitch smiled.

Pru fetched plates and forks, and helped Martha cut three generous slices.

"Yum!" Martha beamed with satisfaction, after tasting a piece. "It's good, even if I do say so myself."

"I'm sure Lauren would be interested in the recipe," Mitch murmured, after swallowing a morsel.

"I got it from that baking book right there." Martha gestured to the large book on the coffee table.

"Jesse's been telling me about this novel." Mitch nodded to the thriller next to the baking book. "What did you think about it, Pru?"

"I liked it so far, but I haven't finished it yet."

"Well, there's plenty of time, now we've caught the killer," Martha said. "And then you and Jesse can have your own book club discussion about it." She chuckled.

"Oh, Martha." She hoped she wasn't blushing.

"Well someone needs to give you two a little push," Martha replied.

"Ruff!" Teddy said in agreement.

THE END

If you sign up to my newsletter, you'll receive a Free and Exclusive short story titled *When Martha Met Her Match.* It's about Martha adopting Teddy from the animal shelter and takes place during **Prowling at the Premiere – A Norwegian Forest Cat Café Cozy Mystery – Book 23**, but it can also be read as a standalone, and it's also the first title in Martha's Senior Sleuthing Club series!

Sign up to my newsletter here:
www.JintyJames.com

If you already receive my newsletter and didn't receive the short story, please email me at

jinty@jintyjames.com and mention the email address you used to sign up with, and I'll send you the link.

Please turn the page for a list of all my books.

TITLES BY JINTY JAMES

Senior Sleuthing Club:

Book Clubs Can Be Fatal – A Senior Sleuthing Club Cozy Mystery – Book 1

Norwegian Forest Cat Café Series:

Purrs and Peril – A Norwegian Forest Cat Café Cozy Mystery – Book 1

Meow Means Murder - A Norwegian Forest Cat Café Cozy Mystery – Book 2

Whiskers and Warrants - A Norwegian Forest Cat Café Cozy Mystery – Book 3

Two Tailed Trouble – A Norwegian Forest Cat Cafe Cozy Mystery – Book 4

Paws and Punishment – A Norwegian Forest Cat Café Cozy Mystery – Book 5

Kitty Cats and Crime – A Norwegian Forest Cat Café Cozy Mystery – Book 6

Catnaps and Clues - A Norwegian Forest Cat Café Cozy Mystery – Book 7

Pedigrees and Poison – A Norwegian Forest Cat Café Cozy Mystery – Book 8

Christmas Claws – A Norwegian Forest Cat Café Cozy Mystery – Book 9

Fur and Felons - A Norwegian Forest Cat Café Cozy Mystery – Book 10

Catmint and Crooks – A Norwegian Forest Cat Café Cozy Mystery – Book 11

Four-Footed Fortune – A Norwegian Forest Cat Café Cozy Mystery – Book 19

Rewards and Revenge – A Norwegian Forest Cat Café Cozy Mystery – Book 20

Catnip and Capture – A Norwegian Forest Cat Café Cozy Mystery – Book 21

Mice and Malice – A Norwegian Forest Cat Café Cozy Mystery – Book 22

Prowling at the Premiere – A Norwegian Forest Cat Café Cozy Mystery – Book 23 (Teddy appears for the first time in this book.)

Maddie Goodwell Series (fun witch cozies)

Spells and Spiced Latte - A Coffee Witch Cozy Mystery - Maddie Goodwell 1

Made in the USA
Coppell, TX
03 October 2023

22364761R00135